# MORGAN

# MORGAN

## Leo P. Kelley

DOUBLEDAY & COMPANY, INC.

GARDEN CITY, NEW YORK

1987

This Large Print Edition contains the complete, unabridged text of the original Doubleday edition.

All of the characters in this book are fictitious, and any resemblance to actual persons, living or dead, is purely coincidental.

Library of Congress Cataloging-in-Publication Data

Kelley, Leo P.
Morgan.

"Garden City large print books."
1. Large type books.   I. Title.
[PS3561.E388M6   1987]      813'.54      87-571
ISBN: 0-385-23987-4

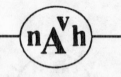

# MORGAN

# ONE

He was the first of the passengers to step down from the stage into the hazy sunshine of the hot June day.

He stood staring and marveling at the many signs that were nailed to the walls of the waterfront buildings that flanked the stage depot.

GET YOUR GOLDWASHER HERE

TOOLS FOR THE DIGGINGS—CHEAP

SHOVELS FOR SALE

A babble of voices shouted for his attention and the attention of the other men leaving the stage.

"Buy firearms to protect yourself in California!" bellowed a thickly mustachioed man. "Out there there's at least one Indian behind every tree, not to mention bush and briar patch! So step right up here, gents, and get your firearms!"

The man who had just stepped down from

the stage grinned. But his grin swiftly vanished as he felt someone suddenly seize his arm.

"Sir," boomed the bespectacled man who had gripped his arm. "I take it you are an argonaut?"

"You take it I'm a what?" he asked the man who had apprehended him.

"Why, a seeker after golden treasure," roared the man in a voice that would have done credit to a hellfire and brimstone preacher. "A man determined to strike it rich in the gold fields of California. In short, an argonaut on his way to see the elephant!"

He shook his arm free. "I'm heading for California to see the elephant, as they say," he admitted. He didn't add that he hoped to strike it rich in the diggings. It didn't seem to him to be necessary to state such an obvious fact.

"Then you'll be wanting—and needing—one of these fine bellows," declared the man, pushing his spectacles up on his nose and lowering his voice as if he were imparting an important secret. "All you have to do, sir, is point it at the ground and squeeze. All the dirt blows away and there you are! Acres of pure gold and all ripe for the picking!"

The merchant's potential customer studied the bellows of various sizes that were suspended by metal S hooks on the wire grid that leaned against the wall of the stage depot.

Someone beside him laughed heartily.

He turned and saw a man of about his own age who was also clean-shaven but much better dressed.

The man said, "Since you're going to California, you should know that California ground doesn't give up its gold all that easily. So save your money, my friend."

"Claim your baggage!" the driver of the stage called down to his passengers.

The man who had been first off the stage looked up at the driver. "Mine's that brown carpetbag."

He caught it when the driver tossed it down to him.

"There's a hotel up that way," the man who had laughed earlier volunteered, pointing to the north. "There's another one down that way." He pointed in the opposite direction. "But if I were you, I'd steer clear of both of them."

"Why?"

"They've got quicks to the north and slows to the south." The man gave another hearty laugh.

"Come again?"

"Quicks," the man repeated. "Fleas. Slows," he added. "Lice."

"I do thank you kindly for the warning."

"Now, you take the place I'm staying. It's as clean as a whistle. Cheap too."

"I'd be much obliged if you'd give me the address of your hotel."

"It's not a hotel. It's just a boardinghouse. The woman who runs it lets rooms by the day or the week. Board is ten dollars extra by the week. Two by the day. Tell you what. I'll do better than give you the address. I'm on my way there right now. Want to walk along?"

"Don't mind if I do."

The late spring sun had set nearly an hour before the stage reached the depot, and now, as the two men walked along the street, twilight deepened.

"Bought your steamer ticket yet?" the man who had volunteered the information about his boardinghouse inquired.

"Not yet. But I'm aiming to do so first thing in the morning."

"By the way, my name's Trask."

"Morgan. I'm pleased to make your acquaintance."

"We turn here."

They entered a narrow alley that was choked with shadows and reeked of rotting garbage. The sound of their feet on the cobblestones was a muted rumble. They had walked some distance down the alley when Trask halted.

"This here's it?" Morgan asked, looking around.

"This is it for you, greenhorn," Trask replied, turning to confront Morgan. "Hand over your money and I won't have to hurt you."

Morgan took a quick step backward, and as he did so someone struck him from behind. The blow landed on the right side of his head and glanced down to thud against his shoulder. As he staggered under its impact, Trask threw a right uppercut that caught Morgan on the chin and sent him arcing backward, his arms flailing into the air. His carpetbag flew from his hand.

*Two!*

The word thundered through Morgan's mind. One behind him. Trask in front of him. He'd been set up!

He regained his balance, and as Trask came lunging toward him, he sent one booted foot flying forward. It caught Trask in the middle of his body, and he doubled up and grabbed his midsection. His breath whooshed out into the deepening darkness.

Morgan spun around. The other unknown man planted a left on his jaw. When he tried to follow up with a right, Morgan put out his bent left arm, blocked the blow, and sent his right fist crashing into the man's face. His attacker careened backward, and as he did so Morgan moved in swiftly and landed another right that sent him stumbling into a wall.

Morgan's fists, one after the other, rammed against his opponent's face and head. The man slammed back against the wall again and then slid down it into a sitting position on the cobblestones. His chin rested on his chest, and his eyes were closed.

Morgan turned quickly to find Trask, who was crouched low with both arms held out in front of him, moving in on him. Something glinted in the little light that spilled into the alley.

Morgan spotted the long-bladed knife in Trask's hand.

"I don't want to cut you," Trask told him. "Or kill you. But I'll do either or both if you don't hand over your passage money plus whatever other money you've got."

Morgan stood his ground as Trask slowly advanced toward him. Then he moved cautiously to one side, circling Trask. Suddenly Trask sprang forward, the knife in his hand pointed directly at Morgan's chest.

Morgan dropped down low, and Trask came

in over his shoulder. Reaching up, Morgan seized Trask's knife hand by the wrist and then, using both hands, slammed it against the wall. The knife clattered on the cobblestones. Morgan put a boot on it.

Trask looked down at the knife and then up at Morgan. "I don't need it," he muttered. "I can take you without it."

"You're right welcome to try," Morgan said coldly.

Trask came in bent over. His left shoulder caught Morgan just below the chest. But Morgan held his ground. He raised both fists and brought them down with fierce force on the back of Trask's neck. Trask grabbed Morgan's shirt but then let go of it as Morgan's blow took effect. He dropped to his knees and then fell facedown on the cobblestones.

Morgan didn't move until he was sure that Trask was out cold. Then he took a step backward. He was about to bend to pick up Trask's knife when he was struck again from behind. The blow caught him at the base of his skull and sent a red sea surging through his brain.

He lost his balance and fell forward, stumbling over the fallen Trask. He turned his head as he fell so that his face wouldn't hit the cobblestones, and he put out both hands to break his fall.

As he hit the cobblestones, he rolled over and then got both feet under him and was on his way up when the second man appeared above him with Trask's knife in his hand. As the knife slashed down, Morgan swung swiftly to the side.

But he had made his move an instant too late. He felt the knife slash the flesh of his right cheek. Before he felt the pain it brought him, he leapt to his feet, sprang forward and sent his left fist slamming against the side of his attacker's head. He raised one knee as the man began to fall and knocked the knife from the man's hand.

Again he waited, looking down at the man lying at his feet. Trask lay not far away. Neither man moved.

Morgan raised his hand and felt his right cheek. Warm. Wet. He withdrew his fingers, sticky with his own blood which he couldn't see because of the near-total darkness that now flooded the alley. He bent, picked up the knife and turned it over in his hand. Then he wiped it on his trousers to clean it of his blood. He looked again at the knife. It might come in handy sometime, he thought. He bent and tucked it inside his right boot. Then he retrieved his carpetbag and made his way back along the alley until he came out into the street.

"Well, now," he said out loud, addressing no one but himself. "That can't count as what a man might call a warm welcome to New York City."

A woman passing by glanced at him in evident alarm.

Automatically he touched the brim of his felt hat to her and smiled.

She covered her mouth with one daintily gloved hand and hurried away down the street.

Well, he thought, she probably wasn't all that accustomed to seeing bloody-faced men pop out at her from dark alleys.

He gingerly fingered his jaw. "Sore as feet in a new pair of boots," he said out loud. But the soreness in his jaw was overwhelmed by the sharp pain in his cheek where Trask's knife had done its damage. As he walked along the crowded streets carrying his carpetbag, he pulled a blue handkerchief from his pocket with his free hand and held it against the wound.

He was surprised to find the streets crowded. Back home in Connecticut, he thought, folks, most of them, would be in bed by now. Most farming folks went to bed with the chickens. Got up with them too. There were chores to be done before breakfast. In fact, there were chores to be done from before first light until after last light.

An odd feeling suddenly swept over him. Was he homesick? he wondered. Well, no. Not exactly. It was more a feeling of— Of what, he asked himself, trying to put a name to the feeling that had swept over him. He finally decided it was one of lonesomeness, the kind a man gets when he finds himself alone in a new place filled with people whose names and faces he doesn't know and who don't even notice him as they go about their business, whatever it might be.

He stopped in front of a doorway framed by two dirty Grecian columns. Above them was a sign: HOTEL.

He went into the lobby and up to the desk. "I'd like to stay the night," he told the thin old man behind the desk.

The desk clerk pushed his green eyeshade up on his forehead and peered at Morgan's bloody face.

"Had me an accident," Morgan told him. "Nothing a little clean water won't fix up just fine."

"Five dollars," said the desk clerk. "In advance."

"*Five* dollars?"

"We're considering raising it to eight," the desk clerk announced smugly. "Lots of young fellers like yourself coming into New York City these days. Big spenders, most of them. On their way to California to hunt for gold, most of them." The desk clerk harrumphed. "Fool's errand, if you ask me."

"Five dollars," Morgan repeated in a low tone. Then he slowly withdrew a leather pouch from a pocket in his trousers, loosened its drawstring and counted out the money.

"Sign here," said the desk clerk, taking the money and shoving a fly-specked ledger toward Morgan.

Morgan signed his name.

"Number twelve. Up those stairs over there, turn right, you can't miss it."

Morgan took the key the man handed him and headed for the stairs.

Once he was inside the room he had rented, he dropped his carpetbag, locked the door behind him and lit the coal oil lamp on the table at the window. He went over to the dresser, above which hung a large mirror, and stared into it, examining the wound on his right cheek.

Then he picked up the porcelain pitcher that sat on top of the dresser and used it to fill the basin next to it with water. He proceeded to clean the caked blood from his wound, using the single towel the hotel had provided.

Fresh blood began to flow from the nearly three-inch-long cut. He washed it away and then pressed the towel against the wound to stop the bleeding.

The man facing him in the mirror was tall, with shoulders almost twice as wide as his hips. His lean frame was taut and tightly muscled.

His face could not be called handsome but it was arresting, composed as it was of sharp angles and flat planes. His eyes were the color of acorns, and there were lines engraved in his skin at the outer edges of his eyes. His hair that buried the tops of his ears and his neck was the color of ripe wheat. His ears lay flat against his head and his lips above his square jaw were neither too thin nor too thick.

The man Morgan saw in the mirror wore a blue cotton shirt, faded homespun trousers that were patched in two places, black mule-eared boots and a battered black felt hat with a rounded crown.

When the blood had dried on his wound, Morgan took off his hat and dropped it on the dresser. Then he went over and sat down on the lumpy bed. He pulled off his boots and socks and then stripped off his clothes. He lay down on the bed, placed his hands behind his head and stared up through the darkness at the ceiling he couldn't see, thinking about the day that was coming and of what it would bring him. Whatever it might be, he hoped it wouldn't include another man with a knife in his hand and murder on his mind.

In the morning, carrying his carpetbag, Morgan left his room and then the hotel. Out on the street, he pulled a folded newspaper clipping from his pocket, unfolded it and read it for what must have been the hundredth time.

It was an advertisement placed by a man named Josiah Green, Esq. It declared that Green was the "authorized agent" for the steamer *Eagle* and it said that Green was selling tickets on the *Eagle* for one hundred and fifty dollars. The *Eagle*, it said, would sail at noon on June 18, 1848, for Chagres on the eastern end of the Isthmus of Panama.

Today! Less than four hours from now . . .

Morgan noted the address of Green's office and, by making inquiries of people he passed, soon found himself in front of it. It was fronted with thick glass on which Green's name was painted in gilded letters. Below the name, also in gilt, were the words *Deeds Drawn—Wills*

*Written.* Above Green's name other words were written in whitewash: *Authorized Steamship Agency.*

Morgan tried the door and found it locked.

Only then did it occur to him that he was too early. New Yorkers, he realized, did not begin their chores as he had done all his life—before dawn. He walked down the street, hunger urging him to search for a restaurant. As he walked he marveled at the tall buildings lining both sides of the street. Many were three and four stories high. One, a shipping firm, was—he counted them—six stories high. High enough, he thought with a grin, to catch clouds on an overcast day.

He found a restaurant and went inside. A waiter wearing a white apron came over to his table.

"What'll it be?"

Morgan knew what he wanted to order. A thick steak, boiled potatoes, two—maybe three —eggs, coffee, some slices of bread thickly spread with butter. But he also knew that the money he had in his leather pouch had to last him from here all the way to the diggings in California. Would it? He didn't know for sure. But he knew there was one way to increase the odds of its lasting in his favor.

"How much do you get for a steak?" he asked the waiter, and the waiter promptly told him.

"That much, huh?" Morgan ran through his list with the waiter and learned the prices of potatoes, eggs, coffee, bread, butter.

"I'll have me an egg and a piece of bread spread with butter," he told the waiter. "A cup of coffee if it's strong stuff."

When his order was placed before him, he devoured it hungrily and then quickly reminded himself that he was not now sitting at the homeplace's kitchen table back in Connecticut. So there would be no second helpings available for the mere asking. He paid his bill and left the restaurant.

He waited for more than an hour in front of Green's office, and at last a man appeared, key in hand.

"Come right in, sir," Green said after introducing himself to Morgan. He ushered Morgan into the office. "I'll be with you in just a moment. Hang your hat right there. Take a seat. Make yourself comfortable."

Morgan hung his hat on a wall peg just inside the door and sat down. Minutes later, Green was ready for him. From behind his desk, the portly steamship agent cleared his throat and beckoned.

When Morgan was seated across from him, Green asked, "Now, then, what can I do for you?"

Morgan pulled the newspaper advertisement from his pocket and placed it on the desk. "I want to buy myself a ticket to get on that boat you mention in there." He pinned the advertisement to the desk with the index finger of his right hand.

"Ah, yes, the *Eagle*," said Green. "A fine ship, that one, with the very finest accommodations."

"I've got the ticket money," Morgan announced. He pulled his leather pouch from his pocket.

"Hold on!"

Morgan looked up at Green, a question in his eyes.

Green was sadly shaking his head. "I'm sorry, I truly am."

"About what?"

"I'm afraid the *Eagle* is fully booked for this trip."

"But I've got to get on!" Morgan exclaimed, half-rising from his chair. He sat back down. "When's the next boat?"

"A fortnight from now."

Morgan looked down at the leather pouch in

his hand. A hotel room, he thought, costs five dollars a night. Five times fourteen . . .

"Wait a moment!" Green cried, his eyes alight. "I've just remembered something." He shuffled through some papers on his desk, then opened a drawer and rummaged through it. "Ah, just as I recalled. Here it is!" He waved a piece of paper in front of Morgan.

Morgan waited, puzzled.

"There was a stateroom reserved only the other day by a Mr.—a Mr.—" Green glanced at the paper in his hand. "By a Mr. Abernathy. It seems that Mr. Abernathy, unfortunate fellow, had only one hundred and twelve dollars, which he gave me as a deposit on his ticket. This is a copy of his receipt. He said he would return with the rest of the money. He hasn't done so."

"I've got one hundred and fifty dollars right in here," Morgan said quickly, holding up his pouch.

"You have, have you?" mused Green, his eyes on the pouch in Morgan's hand. "But I couldn't let you have Mr. Abernathy's stateroom, much as I would like to do so. And it is, I regret to say, the last available one aboard the *Eagle*." He pulled a watch from his vest pocket, snapped it open and squinted at it. "You see, Mr. Abernathy has almost three hours in which to claim his ticket."

"Mr. Green," Morgan said, "I can see the spot you're stuck in. But what if this Mr. Abernathy doesn't show up in time? I mean, that would put you out a hundred and fifty dollars. What's more, that stateroom you've got for sale on board the *Eagle* would just go begging."

Green narrowed his eyes, then smiled broadly. "A very good point, a decidedly significant point. It was, after all, Mr. Abernathy's responsibility to return before this late hour. Yes, indeed it was. As they say, it's the early bird that catches the worm."

"Who catches the steamer ticket?"

"You do, young man! Yes, you, of course. But under the circumstances, I shall have to add a surcharge to the cost of your ticket. Shall we say twenty-five dollars?"

"What for?" Morgan almost shouted at Green.

"Excuse me for a moment." Green rose and spoke to a man who had just entered the office carrying a leather suitcase. "May I help you, young sir?"

"I want to book passage on the *Eagle*," said the man as he closed the door behind him.

"I shall be with you in a moment," Green

told him and sat down again. "The law of supply and demand," he said to Morgan. "If you take my meaning."

Morgan grimly but quickly counted out one hundred and seventy-five dollars and handed it to Green, who thrust it into a drawer in his desk.

He watched Green write on the thin strip of paper that was to be his ticket, and then he accepted it from the agent as if it were a precious nugget of the gold he was going to California to find. He put the ticket in his pocket and was about to rise when a thought occurred to him.

"Mr. Green . . ." He hesitated, wanting to ask the question that was on his mind and at the same time not wanting to ask it in case it would make Green laugh or, worse, sneer at his ignorance.

"Yes?"

"I know my ticket pays for my passage. But I wonder what about meals. Do they by any chance cost extra?"

"Included. All included. And I'm sure you will find them quite to your satisfaction, yes."

"I've got just one more question for you, Mr. Green."

"Ask it."

"About Chagres. I mean about getting from Chagres across the isthmus to Panama City. How might a man go about doing that?"

"You just see Dr. White on board the *Eagle* once you're comfortably settled in your stateroom. He's the man who can arrange for safe passage across the isthmus for you."

"I'll be sure to do that, Mr. Green. Thank you kindly."

"Bon voyage, sir!"

Morgan hurried out of the office. He was halfway down the street, heading for the East River, when he remembered his hat. He had left it hanging on the peg in Green's office. He turned around and headed back to the office.

When he reached it, he stepped inside, reached for his hat and put it on. He was about to leave the office when something Green was saying to the man who had entered the office earlier caught his attention.

". . . will have to add a surcharge to the cost of this ticket."

Morgan stood listening.

Green went on. "I'm sure you won't mind paying a bit extra, considering the fact that Mr. Abernathy's is the last ticket left and there isn't another steamer for a fortnight."

"How much of a surcharge?" asked the man seated at Green's desk.

"Twenty-five dollars or I miss my guess!" Morgan said and strode across the room to the desk. He leaned over it and rested his fists on its surface. "How many other customers have you bamboozled like this?" he asked Green.

"I beg your pardon!" Green exclaimed haughtily.

"Excuse me," said the man seated across from Green, addressing Morgan. "When I've concluded my business with this gentleman, you may then—"

Morgan interrupted him. "When you've finished with this shyster, you'll be skinned clean as a caught coon!" Morgan hadn't taken his eyes from Green's face. Now he held out his right hand, palm up. "I want my twenty-five dollars back!"

"See here!" declared Green's customer. "I—"

"You snap that trap of yours shut, mister, and give a listen to what I've got to say."

Morgan quickly explained to the man the gambit Green had used on him and how he was now using the same gambit again.

"Why, that is outrageous!" cried the suddenly indignant customer.

"The way I conduct my business," declared Green as confidently as he could under Morgan's stony stare, "is my business."

"And my business," Morgan said harshly, "at this particular minute is to get back that twenty-five dollars you took from me. I'm willing to pay the price you advertised. But not a single cent more!"

Green rose from his chair. "I'll summon an officer of the law. He will know how to deal with a hoodlum like you!"

Morgan raised his eyebrows in mock surprise and then tilted his hat back on his head. "I never once before have ever been mistaken for a hoodlum, Mr. Green, and that's a fact. But I guess I can understand how that might happen.

"A man like me, I get provoked, why, there's just no telling what I might do. Why, I might take a notion to bust up this fancy desk of yours, and then, if I still didn't get my money back, I might try busting *you* up next. Now, I can understand how anyone watching me fuss who didn't know what put the burr in my britches would mistake me for a hoodlum for certain."

Morgan slammed a fist down on the desk, causing it to shudder.

Green sat down heavily. He opened his desk drawer, counted out twenty-five dollars and handed the money to Morgan. "Now, get out of my office!" he shouted.

"Not just yet," Morgan said quietly. "I want to see you sell this here gent a hundred-and-fifty-dollar ticket for a stateroom on the *Eagle*. Him and me are going to be shipmates, and the way I see it, shipmates have got to look out for one another in a storm."

Green, looking as if he were about to weep, made out the second ticket and handed it to the man, who promptly paid for it. Then he and Morgan left the office of the obviously aggrieved agent.

Outside, the man put down his leather suitcase and held out his hand to Morgan. "I want to thank you for your intervention in that rather ugly matter. I was perfectly willing to believe his story about there being but a single stateroom left on the *Eagle*, and that one reserved. Why, I would have paid *two* hundred and fifty dollars to get on the *Eagle*."

"A penny saved is a penny earned, or so I've heard tell," Morgan said as he shook the man's hand. "So's twenty-five dollars."

The man laughed and then said, "Well, we might as well head for the river and the steamer."

"I suppose it won't hurt to be first on board, now will it?" Morgan said with a grin.

"Allow me to introduce myself," the man said as they walked toward the East River. "My name is Cassius Jamieson, Jr."

"Shad Morgan."

"Shad? Unusual name. I don't recall ever having heard it before."

"Sure, you have. Shad's short for Shadrach."

"Oh, I see."

"Maybe you don't. My ma she was a Bible-reading woman. She tried to live what she read as best as ever she could before she passed on. Tried to bring it all to life, you might say. So that's how I come by my name—Ma plucked it right out of the good book. She did the same with both my brothers' names, too. Gideon, he came along first, and Jonah came not long after me."

"I've got no brothers or sisters," Jamieson volunteered, and Morgan thought the man sounded sad as he stated the fact. "But having none had its advantages," Jamieson added more cheerfully. "Everything came my way as a result."

Morgan was not a man to ask personal questions of even close friends and certainly not of strangers, so he said nothing as they walked along, but he covertly examined his companion.

Jamieson was dressed nattily in a three-piece suit. His white shirt had a high starched collar, and his gray tie was as crisp as his shirt. There wasn't a trace of lint on his derby hat. Morgan looked down at Jamieson's polished black shoes. He'd expected to see spats covering them, but Jamieson wasn't wearing any.

The man had an eager, almost boyish look about him, Morgan noticed. The skin of his face was as smooth as a plum. His eyes were blue, and his neatly barbered and pomaded hair was brown.

"Look over there, Shad!" Jamieson said, pointing. "Now, we could use some of those tasty items to spice up our diet during the voyage."

Morgan glanced at the store Jamieson had pointed out. Its huge windows were heaped high with delicacies of all kinds. Pickles, gingerbread cakes, chocolate cookies, chili sauce in tall jars and more kinds of cheeses and canned goods than could be counted.

"Come on, Shad," Jamieson said as he headed for the store.

Morgan shrugged and followed him inside to find Jamieson already at the counter, where a fat man behind it was making a list of the items Jamieson wanted to purchase. When they left the store some time later, they were loaded down with boxes full of canned goods.

Struggling with their heavy loads, they finally arrived, sweating, at the wharf where the *Eagle* was berthed. The gangplank wasn't in place, so they piled Jamieson's provisions on the wharf and sat down on them to rest.

Jamieson began to pull cans out of one of his boxes to examine them. "Mustard pickle," he declared and waved a can in the air. "Canned lamb. Sardines. And here is the pièce de résistance," he added, holding up a large can. "Genuine Indian chutney. We can have ourselves a fine picnic with all this, Shad," he declared happily.

"Picnic?"

"Well, we are going on a kind of picnic, aren't we? First the trip down to Chagres, during which we won't have to lift a finger in labor, and then across the isthmus to Panama City and then a smooth sail up to San Francisco. Why, Shad, this gold rush is the biggest picnic of the century! And when our fortunes are made, why, we'll just gather up all our gold and come right back home!"

Jamieson's last word echoed in Morgan's

mind. *Home.* Already the Connecticut farm on which he had been born and raised seemed very far away to him. Would he even be able to remember it, he wondered, when he was actually a whole continent—three thousand miles—away from it? But he'd come back to it. To Pa and Jonah and Gideon and Gideon's wife, Nan, and their little girl, Grace.

And when he finally did come home, he would bring gold, lots of it, he vowed to himself. Gold that they all would share as surely as they had all shared the hard work on the farm and the good life it offered them. Morgan thought with quiet pride of the way the decision had been made. Gideon had wanted to go to California. He had talked for months of heading west to Missouri and then taking the overland route to the diggings. But there were Nan and Grace to consider and some doubt about whether either of them could stand the rigors of the journey. And Nan didn't want Gideon to go alone. Pa was getting old, and even if he was still as tough as hickory, the years had begun to take their toll on him. But they all agreed that they wanted to try for their fair share of all that California gold.

Jonah also wanted to go, but his father had picked Morgan as the one to represent them all in the diggings. If Shad did well, Pa had promised, Jonah could follow him to California.

They had all scraped together, from any and every source available to them, the money Morgan would need to make the trip.

Some had come from the money they had saved for the spring planting, some from Gideon who said he could postpone buying a bull for a spell. Jonah had insisted his old rifle needed only a new firing pin to be almost as good as new, so the money he'd put aside to buy a new rifle could go into Morgan's leather pouch.

Morgan's father's contribution came from a mattress that only he had known contained anything other than straw. Nan emptied the little chamois bag she kept in her dresser drawer next to the small sack of lavender and gave the money it contained to Morgan. The rest came from the tiny bank account Pa had been trying hard to build up over the years.

The total had come to almost five hundred dollars, a small fortune. It was more money than any one of them had ever seen in a single place at a single time.

And so Morgan had said his good-byes—Nan had shed a tear or two, which she had tried to hide—and then he had boarded the stage for

New York City. Now here he was, he thought, the first part of his journey completed, the second about to begin.

He stepped back and stared at the steamer. The *Eagle* had three masts, and on each of them members of the crew were checking the rigging and unfurling the sails. An American flag was suspended from a pole jutting out from the mast nearest the stern of the ship. Just in front of the stern mast stood the tall galvanized smokestack. The ship sat high in the water, rocking gently in an occasional swell.

He turned his attention to the men waiting on the wharf. Like him, he supposed, they were not heading out to California only for gold. There was more to it than that; at least there was for him, he knew, and, he suspected, for most, if not all, of the other waiting passengers as well.

There was freedom to be found out there in the West as well as gold. The frontier was a place where a man would have room to stretch his horizons, where his eyes could study new sights, where he could roam at will and meet each new day with a dare. Excitement surged through him as he thought of the future—his future.

"Here comes the gangplank!" Jamieson

yelled. He took off his derby and tossed it high into the air. *"Let's go, Shad!"*

Hastily they gathered up the boxes of canned foods, suitcase and carpetbag and joined the throng already pressing toward the gangplank that was being set in place against the side of the *Eagle.* It took them almost ten minutes to finally reach the steamer's deck.

Men were shouting, laughing, clapping one another on the back as if to celebrate some suddenly won victory.

In the midst of all the clamor, a white-coated steward answered questions as best he could in the deafening din.

Morgan dropped the boxes he had been carrying onto the deck and shouldered his way through the crowd. When he reached the steward, he cupped his hands around his mouth and yelled a question.

"Which way to our staterooms?"

The steward shouted a reply. Morgan didn't hear the man's answer so he turned his head, and the steward shouted into his ear.

A simple reply. The passengers would be shown to their quarters once the ship was away from the wharf.

Morgan returned to Jamieson and relayed the news.

Together they stood at the railing and watched the last of the men climb the gangplank. Minutes later the gangplank was withdrawn and the lines were cast off. The harsh sound of the iron anchor being raised brought a collective cheer from the throats of the assembled passengers, as did the metallic rumble of the boilers below deck as they were fired up.

Then the steamer was moving away from the wharf and heading down the East River toward the open ocean.

Morgan turned, and when he spotted the steward, motioned to Jamieson to follow him and then he headed in the man's direction.

The steward agreed to show them to what he called their accommodations. Morgan and Jamieson, carrying boxes and luggage, followed him to a hatch in the center of the deck. The steward bent and lifted the hinged hatch cover. He climbed down a wooden ladder that led below deck, with Morgan and Jamieson at his heels. He headed down a long narrow passageway and stopped when he reached the ship's hold. In the hold stood a forest of tiered wooden racks, each one consisting of three bunks.

"There must be some mistake," Jamieson told the steward. "We paid for staterooms, not steerage."

"This here's what you paid for," the steward stated flatly.

Jamieson glanced at Morgan, who was studying the smirk on the steward's face.

Morgan put down the boxes he had been carrying. Jamieson followed his example. Morgan put down his carpetbag, Jamieson, his suitcase.

"We paid for staterooms," Morgan said bluntly to the steward. "We want them."

"Mister," said the steward, "take your complaints somewheres else. Maybe we have a preacher on board. Maybe you can ferret him out and tell him your tale of woe."

Morgan reached out swiftly and seized a fistful of the steward's white coat. He jerked the man toward him. "You heard what I said. Now you just mosey along and show us the way to our staterooms."

The steward tried and failed to pry open Morgan's clenched fingers. "I told you the truth," he whined. "I swear I did! There aren't any staterooms on the *Eagle*—only these bunks. The *Eagle* was a coastal freighter till the gold rush started. Then her owner converted her to carry passengers. That's why the captain won't let me take anybody below deck till we're out in open water!"

"So nobody can leave the ship once he sees

this," Morgan muttered, waving a hand at the racks.

The steward, his eyes wide with fright, nodded and swallowed hard.

Morgan gave a snort of disgust and released him.

As the steward bolted, a shouting crowd of men stormed into the hold.

"If we want bottom bunks," Morgan said to Jamieson, "we'd best be about scrambling for them."

They both picked up their boxes and luggage and ran to the nearest of the three-tiered racks and sat down on lower bunks facing one another.

"What was it you were saying not so far back, Cass, about going on a picnic?"

Jamieson shook his head, and a rueful smile parted his lips.

Morgan nodded soberly. "Some picnic this trip is turning out to be. By the sharp feel of the boards in this here bunk of mine, I reckon I'll have me a hole or two in my hide long before we step ashore in Chagres."

# TWO

A loud report roared through the hold of the ship.

It awoke Morgan, who quickly reached under his bunk's ticking and withdrew his revolver. It was a .31-caliber five-shot Colt Wells Fargo model. It had a three-inch barrel and a silver-plated guard and straps.

*"Don't shoot!"*

Morgan recognized Jamieson's voice, but in the darkness he could barely make out Jamieson's body as the man tried to get out of his bunk.

Another loud report drowned the faint echoes of the first. Men began to shout as they jumped down from their bunks and proceeded to bump into one another and curse the darkness and each other.

Morgan was up, his revolver in his steady hand.

Suddenly a tier of bunks was overturned by the milling mob. It crashed against its neighbor that was only three feet from it. Vivid oaths filled the darkness as men fought to free themselves from the trap that the fallen rack had become.

Someone lit a coal oil lamp.

Morgan blinked in the sudden yellow light that seeped through the hold. Only one thought occupied his mind. Find the man with the gun!

"Shad!" Jamieson cried as he got out of his bunk. "What did you shoot for?"

Morgan shook his head, his eyes darting about the hold. "Wasn't me." That second shot, he thought. I was awake when it was fired. But I didn't see any flame from a gun barrel.

"Smells like a den of skunks died in here!" someone shouted.

Morgan realized that the man was right. The hold reeked. But of what?

Another sharp report sounded throughout the hold. Jamieson ran a few steps and then turned back to look at his bunk.

Morgan lowered his gun and grinned at Jamieson. "There goes your picnic, Cass."

Jamieson walked back to his bunk, bent and pulled out the boxes of canned goods he had stored beneath it. "Whew!"

Morgan deposited his revolver in his carpetbag beneath his bunk. He stared down at the three cans that had exploded. Then he looked up at Jamieson. "Canning's not what you could call a perfect science, Cass. Maybe it's best that those things blew up on you. You might have been poisoned."

"I thought I was being smart, Shad. Buying all those things, I mean. But you were the smart one. You didn't waste your money on this—" Jamieson waved a hand to indicate the exploded cans that contained putrid meat.

"It wasn't so much a matter of me being smart, Cass, as it was a matter of thrift. Were I a rich man, I'd've bought some of those dainties, too, just as quick as a cat can catch a crow."

"Hey, mister!" a man yelled at Jamieson. "Move that mess of yours the hell out of here. This ain't no pigsty!"

"I'll give you a hand," Morgan volunteered and proceeded to pull on his trousers and then his boots.

When Jamieson was dressed, he and Morgan carried the boxes up on deck and there, in the thin light of false dawn, began to pitch the cans overboard.

"Shad, look down there!"

Morgan looked down at the ocean. At first he saw nothing. Then he saw the fin of a sleek gray shark slice through the water not far from the steamer.

"That fish sure looks mean," commented a beefy man as he came up to stand at the railing beside Morgan. "Look at those teeth he's got," he exclaimed as the shark surfaced. He took a can from one of the boxes and threw it at the shark. The shark's jaws opened wide and the can disappeared between them.

A second shark appeared.

"Watch this, boys!" said the man, reaching for another can.

Morgan's arm shot out and his hand seized the man's wrist. "Drop it!"

The man turned to face Morgan, anger in his eyes. "Let me loose!"

"Drop it!" Morgan repeated. When the man didn't drop the can he was holding, Morgan twisted his arm behind him and then forced it up between the man's shoulderblades.

The man let out a cry of pain. He dropped the can, which fell to the deck.

Morgan released him.

"What for did you do that?" the man muttered, rubbing his wrist.

"I don't have any fondness for sharks," Morgan answered. "But neither do I have any feud with them. What do you think would happen to a fish if one of those cans exploded inside its belly? Now, the way I see it, those sharks don't have enough sense not to swallow those cans. But you, mister, I reckon you got enough sense not to feed them fare that won't do them any good and just might do them permanent harm."

As the beefy man stalked away muttering, Morgan bent, picked up a box and hurled it overboard. He did the same with the remaining boxes. "Well, that's been seen to. Now there's nothing to do but wait for breakfast."

"I'm not so sure I want any breakfast," Jamieson said. "I couldn't eat any of that salt pork they served us last night. It was slimy, most of it, and what wasn't was turning green."

"You'd best eat to keep up your strength, Cass. We're only two days out and we got a good many more days to go before we reach Chagres. You stop eating for the rest of this trip and likely as not the captain'll be saying a few holy words over you before he turns you over to those sharks down there."

Jamieson glanced down to where the two sharks still knifed through the water. Then he sat on the deck and leaned back against the railing. Morgan continued to stand, staring out over the open ocean, the light wind cool on his bare chest.

"I talked to one of our fellow passengers yesterday," Jamieson said. "He's leaving the ship at

Charleston. He said he wasn't going on even if he had to walk all the way back home. He's been sick since the first day out due to the awful food they've been serving us."

Morgan absently ran a finger along the scabbed wound on his cheek.

Jamieson happened to look up as he did so. "What happened, Shad?"

Morgan told him about his fight with Trask and Trask's companion in crime.

"Why, you could have been killed instead of just cut up in that fight!"

"Reckon so."

Jamieson raised his knees, propped his elbows on them and cupped his hands beneath his chin. "I guess the grass isn't always greener on the other side of the fence," he mused.

"Sometimes it just looks that way," Morgan remarked, wondering what Jamieson was getting at.

"I gave up studying to be a lawyer to head for California's green grass," Jamieson said. "Right now Harvard seems a world away from here."

Morgan looked down at him. "You were being schooled at Harvard University?"

Jamieson nodded. "It wasn't my idea though. It was my father's—Cassius Jamieson, Sr. He's a lawyer and he loves the law. He wanted me to follow in his footsteps. But I didn't want to be a lawyer."

"What do you want to be?"

"I guess that's my main trouble. I don't really know. I've never found anything I could really care deeply about."

Morgan turned his head and stared out over the ocean that was whitecapped now. "A man's got to have something to care about. It can be just about anything, I reckon. A woman. Some kind of business he gets himself into. His religion, if he's got one. It's what gets him out of bed in the morning and lets him sleep sound come night."

"What about you, Shad? What do you care about?"

"Me? I reckon with me it's the land I care about. Now, I don't mean to hand any nosegays to that Connecticut soil I've left behind me for the time being. It's as chock full of rocks as a chicken's craw is of gravel. It takes a pure delight in breaking a plow, not to mention the back of any man who sets out to fight it. But it's there, Cass. The thing is the land is there and it's yours. You were born on it and you soon find out you've put your roots down into it."

"Why did you leave it if it means so much to you?"

"Why? That's an easy question to come up with an answer to. Gold. That's why I left it. To find some gold out in California so that me and my family won't have a hardscrabble time of it all the rest of our days.

"Now, you take my brother, Gideon. He's married himself a fine woman—her name's Nan —and the two of them they have a little girl not yet four. Gideon never did own a pair of pants that didn't wind up patched."

Morgan caught Jamieson's glance at his own patched trousers. He grinned. "I reckon you can see what I'm getting at as plain as day. Well, that's been the way of it till now. Nan wears mostly homespun. Sometimes calico. She's never said so, but I reckon she wouldn't turn down a silk dress for Sundays if she ever found it within her means. Then there's Pa. Worked hard all his life he has and never did have a real holiday of any kind. And Jonah, he wants more schooling than he's likely to get, things being how they are with us. So that's why I left, Cass. I had me a whole lot of good reasons."

"What do you want for yourself, Shad?"

Without hesitation Morgan answered, "The chance to live my life without owing any man nor having to do any man's bidding."

"That's not much."

"Why, Cass, you're as wrong as wrong can be! Man, that's *everything!*"

"You've never thought of turning back?"

"Nope. Can't. Got people depending on me."

Jamieson shook his head, lowering his eyes to the deck. "Some of the passengers are saying that some men have never made it up the Chagres River to Panama City. They say men have died on the Chagres."

"I've heard the talk. Maybe it's true talk and maybe it isn't. If it is true, well, there's nothing for it but to take on the trial and get through it the best way we can." Morgan looked up at the sky. "Looks like we won't see the sun today. Those clouds look close enough to catch hold of. Wind's rising too."

"You're quite right on that score, my young friend," said a man wearing a Prince Albert coat as he joined Morgan and Jamieson at the railing. "We're heading into a storm. I can read the signs, having traveled on this ship before."

"You've been aboard the *Eagle* before?" Jamieson asked the man as he got to his feet.

The man's face broke into a broad smile. "Twice before. A matter of business. And it's business, if I may say so, that has prompted me to take the liberty of interrupting your conversation."

"What business do you happen to be in?" Morgan asked the man.

"Permit me to introduce myself. I am Dr. White. Perhaps the steamship agent in New York—"

"He did mention your name," Morgan said, remembering. "He said you were the fellow to see about our passage up the Chagres River."

"Quite right," Dr. White said, his smile broadening. "Since I have not had the pleasure of offering my services as yet to you two gentlemen, I thought I'd just step up and—"

"How much?" Morgan asked.

"That depends, my friend, on how you want to travel. Now, you can go upriver by dugout. Or you can haul a towboat filled with your provisions. Or you can buy mules to carry your provisions and yourselves."

"What's the best way?" Morgan asked.

"I would recommend a dugout, which can be poled upriver by several experienced and trustworthy Indians."

"Beats walking or mule riding, does it, this dugout you're talking about?" Morgan asked.

"So they tell me, although I've never actually

made the trip myself, to be quite candid about it," answered Dr. White, still smiling.

"How much?" Morgan asked a second time.

"Twenty-five dollars. Apiece."

Jamieson reached into his pocket and came up with a small purse. He snapped it open, pulled out several bills and handed them to Dr. White.

"Thank you, sir," said Dr. White as he pocketed the money and glanced at Morgan.

"Can't a man make it on his own?" Morgan asked.

"Of course he can—or he might, at any rate," Dr. White replied pleasantly. "But not all the Indians are friendly. Those who are can help a man avoid the dangers of the five-day journey."

"I'll pay your passage," Jamieson said quickly. "My ticket would have cost me an extra twenty-five dollars if it hadn't been for you, so—"

"No," Morgan said, shaking his head. He pulled out his leather pouch, loosened its drawstring and counted out twenty-five dollars, which he handed to Dr. White.

"Your names, gentlemen?" Dr. White inquired. He took a small notebook from his pocket and the stub of a pencil. When he had their names, he wet the tip of the pencil on his tongue and jotted them down in his notebook.

"We'll meet again in Chagres, gentlemen, if not before," he said amiably. He gave a slight bow and then strode away down the deck.

"I'd say it's about breakfast time," Morgan commented. "It is, I mean, if my stomach's to be trusted. And it is. It tells time better than any clock ever invented. Let's go, Cass."

Without waiting for an answer, Morgan headed for the hatch. Before he reached it, a light rain began to fall. He quickened his pace and hurriedly descended the ladder.

When Jamieson caught up with him in the hold, he had put on his shirt and was buttoning it.

Jamieson sat down on his bunk and looked up at Morgan. "I didn't know you carried a gun," he remarked. He reached under his bunk and took a bottle of whiskey from his suitcase. He drank from it and then offered it to Morgan, who shook his head.

"I didn't know you were packing a bottle, Cass. Seems like there are still some things we have to find out about each other. You all set for breakfast?"

"You go on. I'll join you later."

Morgan made his way out of the hold and

down the passageway. When he reached the crowded dining room, he looked about for an empty place on one of the benches flanking the long wooden tables.

"You're welcome to sit in this here spot, sonny," said an elderly bearded man.

"Thank you kindly," Morgan said and sat down beside the man.

"Where's your mate?" the old man asked him. "He didn't blow up along with his canned goods, now, did he?"

Morgan grinned. "Not likely. But those explosions sure did put a scare into him. Understandable when you consider how much like gunshots they sounded."

The steward appeared and put a plate and a cup of coffee in front of Morgan, who looked down and ruefully shook his head. Among the beans wriggled tiny insects.

"Pick 'em out," the old man advised him. "It's a chore, I admit, seeing as how there are about two bugs to every bean. But what else is a feller to do?"

Morgan spent several minutes searching out and then squeezing the insects between his thumb and index finger. His companion passed him a basket that had been resting in the middle of the table.

He took a piece of pilot bread from it. Before placing the bread on his plate, he brushed away the weevils that had begun to spin their lacy webs in it.

"Most of the fellers on board," said the old man through a mouthful of beans, "have taken to complaining about the food. I tell 'em they got nothing to complain about. Where else could they get served fresh meat three times a day?" He pointed at an insect crawling on his plate, let out a roar of laughter and slapped his thigh.

Morgan reached for his cup of coffee to wash down the taste of the food he had just eaten. But the table suddenly tilted and the cup slid away from him. He managed to grab it before it slid off the table.

"The sea's getting kind of rough," observed his companion.

As if to confirm the man's judgment, the table tilted in the opposite direction. Morgan fought to maintain his balance on the bench beneath him.

Plates suddenly crashed to the floor and broke. The basket of pilot bread soared through the air and hit the bulkhead. As the ship righted itself, Morgan got to his feet.

"I'll pass up the coffee," he told his companion. "Hope I can keep these beans down. I can feel them churning around deep down inside me. Or maybe it's some bugs I missed."

As he headed for the door, he collided with the steward, who came running into the dining room.

"The captain says we're heading into a hurricane!" the steward announced at the top of his voice. "He says all passengers are to go to the hold and stay there till we ride out this weather!"

Morgan returned to the hold and sat down on his bunk. Across from him, Jamieson had assumed a sitting position on his bunk, his back propped against his folded pillow. In his hand was his nearly half-empty bottle of whiskey.

"You want breakfast, you'd best hurry up after it," Morgan advised him.

Jamieson merely shook his head and drank from his bottle.

"The captain sent word we've got us a hurricane on our hands, Cass."

"Does he think we'll sink?" Jamieson giggled.

"Didn't say so."

Jamieson offered his bottle to Morgan, who shook his head.

Men began to crowd into the hold and climb into their bunks. One man began to groan as the ship heaved sharply to one side and then to the other.

The tiered racks that held the bunks began to slide along the deck. Some of the men tried to hold them in place. Suddenly the bow of the ship shot up into the air, sending the racks sliding backward toward the passageway.

Morgan sprang from his bunk as it began to topple and leapt out of the way of another rack that was rapidly bearing down on him. Stepping swiftly to one side, he managed to escape from the path of the rack, which careened past him to crash against the bulkhead behind him.

". . . sick."

Morgan caught only Jamieson's last word. The rest of what he had said had been lost in the loud uproar created by the crashing of the racks as they collided and overturned and by the shouts of the men who were trying to avoid being struck by them.

He turned to find Jamieson, one hand over his mouth, the other holding his bottle of whiskey, struggling out of his bunk.

He put out a hand to help Jamieson, but Jamieson, ignoring it or not seeing it, fell to the deck, smashing his bottle as he did so.

His face, Morgan noted, was as pale as frost. His cheeks bulged. He staggered toward the passageway. But before he could reach it, a rack toppled over as the ship lurched violently to one side. It knocked Jamieson to his knees. He scrambled hurriedly to his feet, his hand still covering his mouth.

Morgan shouted his name as Jamieson bolted into the passageway.

Dodging tumbling racks and shouting men, Morgan made slow progress toward the passageway. When he was finally in it, Jamieson was nowhere in sight.

He ran down the passageway. As he passed the ladder leading to the upper deck, the heavy rain pelting through the open hatch soaked his shirt. When he was halfway to the room where he had just eaten, the ship rocked sharply to one side, throwing him against a bulkhead. He recovered his balance and ran on.

Jamieson, he discovered, had disappeared. A thought suddenly crossed his mind. He tried to dismiss it. Jamieson wouldn't be that foolish, he told himself. But where else could the man have gone?

He raced back along the passageway, his arms thrust out at right angles to his body to keep himself from being thrown against the passageway bulkheads. He finally reached the ladder leading to the main deck. He started to climb it, only to find his way blocked by one of the steamer's crewmen.

"Get back!" the man shouted down at Morgan above the roar of the wind that was funneling down through the hatch. "I've got to close this hatch before we all drown!"

"Did you see a man come up this ladder a little while ago?" Morgan yelled up at the crewman.

"No!"

"Get out of my way! A friend of mine might be out there on deck!"

"If he is out there," the crewman yelled, "he's a dead friend!" He continued struggling to close the hatch.

Morgan seized him by the shoulder and shoved him to one side. He climbed through the open hatch and stood on the deck, swaying in the strong wind and because the deck was tilting beneath his boots. He crouched on the deck as a wave that was half as high as the main mast towered above the steamer and then crashed down upon it. A third of the deck went underwater as the ship tilted at a precarious angle. Overhead the mid-morning sky was almost black. Rain poured down from it in torrents, soaking Morgan to the skin. He couldn't see more than a few feet in any direction. He held tightly to the rough edge of the hatch housing and yelled Jamieson's name.

Only the howling wind answered him.

"Cass!" he yelled again, looking about him in every direction.

A moment later he spotted Jamieson kneeling on the deck, his arms wrapped around the iron railing that ringed the steamer's deck.

He turned his head and yelled to the crewman on the ladder. "There's a man out here. I'm going to try—"

The crewman slammed the hatch cover shut, bloodying Morgan's fingers as he did so.

A huge wave washed over Jamieson, flooding the deck. His body lay limply on the deck after the wave passed.

"Cass! Hold on!"

The wind whipped Morgan, and the rain tried to blind him. He knew he couldn't remain where he was. He needed some kind of anchor, something to hold on to to keep from being swept overboard. He had to act fast, he knew, because Jamieson's slack body indicated that he wouldn't be able to maintain his hold on the railing much longer.

Desperately Morgan looked around him, blinking the rain out of his eyes. The bare expanse of deck stretched out all around him.

He looked up. The sails had been secured. Ropes that had ripped free of the rigging whirled in the wild wind. The stern mast, Morgan estimated, was a good ten yards from where he crouched. An idea occurred to him. Could he do it?

He decided to risk a try. With one last glance to the left to make sure that Jamieson was still clinging to the railing, Morgan rose and sprinted forward as the steamer pitched unpredictably beneath his boots. He almost overshot his mark, but he managed to wrap his left arm around the mast as he slid along the wet deck. He immediately began to climb the mast.

When he reached the rigging he halted, and then, reaching down, he pulled the knife from his boot and began to cut through one of the thick ropes that bound the sail to the crossbar.

It took him several minutes to cut through it, but at last he had a length of rope that he hoped would be long enough for his purpose. He returned the knife to his boot and began his descent. When he felt the slippery deck beneath him once again, he placed the mast between himself and Jamieson.

"Cass!"

He had to shout the name again before Jamieson's head rose slightly and turned groggily in his direction.

"I'll toss you this rope!" Morgan yelled to him. He held the rope high above his head, his chest pressed against the mast and his knees gripping it tightly.

He coiled the rope tightly and then threw it in Jamieson's direction. His effort failed because at the very moment that he tossed the rope, a gigantic wave rocked the ship and the rope came flying back toward him.

He tried a second time. On his third try, Jamieson managed to catch the end of the rope.

"Hold tight to that rope!" Morgan yelled to him. "I'll pull you over here!" With his chest still pressed against the mast and his knees still gripping it, he began to pull in the rope.

Jamieson came away from the railing. He rolled over and over on the deck as the ship heaved. But he kept his hands fisted around the rope, which Morgan continued to pull in.

Morgan gave one final tug on the rope.

Jamieson's fists struck the mast. He lost his grip on the rope and began to slide back across the sloping deck toward the railing.

Morgan quickly reached out and grabbed Jamieson's shirt. He pulled Jamieson toward him and then, just as the cloth of Jamieson's shirt shredded in his hands, he succeeded in pulling him around behind the mast.

He kneeled, shook his wet hair out of his eyes as rain streamed down his face, and pulled Jamieson up into a sitting position with his back braced against the mast. As the rain continued to hammer down upon them and the raging wind whipped them, he looped the rope around the mast. He pulled both ends of it toward him, brought them under Jamieson's arms and tied the rope around the man's chest. He held the loose end of the rope in both hands, looking from it to the hatch in the distance. The remaining length of rope was, he realized, too short to do the job he had in mind.

Squinting up into the downpour, he knew what he had to do. He dropped the useless length of rope and began to climb the mast a second time, his knife clenched between his teeth.

When he reached the crossbar, he wrapped his legs around the mast, held tightly to it with his left hand, leaned out and, taking his knife in his right hand, began to cut through another rope that was helping to hold the sail in place. As he withdrew the length of rope he had severed, part of the sail dropped free. The wind seized it and threw it into his face. The wet slap of the canvas took him by surprise, and he almost lost his hold on the mast. He shoved the furiously flapping canvas away from him and, after placing his knife in his boot, began his descent.

When he stood once more on the deck, he tied one end of the rope to the mast just above Jamieson's head. As he worked, Jamieson said something Morgan didn't hear because the wind whirled the words away.

When he had the rope fastened securely to the mast, he dropped to the deck and deliberately flattened himself against it. That way, he reasoned, he would make less of a target for the wind's wild fingers. Using his elbows and knees to propel himself forward, he quickly made his way across the deck toward the hatch, clutching the free end of the rope in his right hand.

Once he reached the hatch, he tried in vain to pry it open. He pulled his knife from his boot and used it on the hatch cover, but to no avail. He returned the knife to his boot. The rain must have caused the wooden cover to swell, he guessed. It wouldn't come up.

*It wouldn't come up.*

An idea flashed through his mind. If the hatch cover wouldn't come up, maybe it would go down—maybe it could be made to go down.

He sat on the deck with the rope between his teeth. He placed both hands, palms down, on the deck behind him and began to pound his boot heels against the hatch cover. He kept up the relentless tattoo for what seemed to him like hours. But before those hours ended, the hatch cover began to yield.

He renewed his efforts despite the fact that the bones in his heels had become screaming centers of sharp pain. Finally he succeeded in shattering the hatch cover. He leaned forward and ripped away the remains of the splintered wood.

Then he wrapped the free end of the rope around the two-inch-tall base of the hatch and knotted it in place. He flattened himself against the deck again and made his way back toward Jamieson, holding tightly to the taut rope that now stretched between the hatch cover and the mast.

When he reached Jamieson, he untied the rope that held him lashed to the mast, realizing as he did so that Jamieson was no longer conscious.

He kneeled on the deck, hoisted Jamieson and tossed him over his shoulder. Holding tightly to the rope with his right hand, he crawled back across the deck, head down against the wind and rain, until he reached the open hatch.

Slowly he began to descend the ladder, one careful step at a time. When he reached the bottom of the ladder, he bent and lowered the unconscious Jamieson to the deck. Then he sat down, unmindful of the rain-drenched passageway, leaned back against the bulkhead and rested his crossed arms on his bent knees. He dropped his head on his arms, dimly aware of the shouting men moving about in the passageway.

Minutes later he raised his head. Above him on the ladder a crewman was covering the open hatch with a tarpaulin. He looked down at Jamieson, who lay at his feet. He thought he had seen Jamieson's eyelids flicker.

He reached out, gripped Jamieson's shoulder and gently shook the man.

Jamieson's eyes snapped open. He looked about fearfully, tried to rise, fell back.

"You're safe now," Morgan told him.

"Shad—Shad, thanks, I—"

"Just you take it easy now, Cass."

"You must be crazy, mister."

Morgan looked up at the wide-eyed man who had just spoken to him.

"I mean," the awed man continued, "to go

out there in this hurricane that must have got loose from hell itself. Why in the name of God's great creation did you go and do a crazy thing like that?"

"This man's a friend of mine," Morgan answered, indicating Jamieson. "He needed help."

Morgan's questioner shook his head as if Morgan's explanation made no sense to him at all.

# THREE

On a muggy morning more than a month after the storm, Morgan stood with Jamieson on the beach at Chagres, which was ringed with more than a score of reed huts thatched with palm leaves, and watched the *Eagle* leave the harbor and steam north.

"Good-bye and good riddance!" Jamieson muttered and then angrily damned the ship and its crew. "I'm not the least bit sorry to see the last of that floating pesthouse."

Morgan looked up at the ruins that stood on a slight elevation above them.

"That was a fortress named San Lorenzo," Jamieson volunteered. "I read about it and this place in a book."

"It looks to be garrisoned by nothing but goats these days," Morgan observed, his eyes on the animals roaming through and around the ruins.

"Some three hundred men died in it when it was attacked by the pirate Morgan in the seventeenth century. By the way, was he, perchance, an ancestor of yours, Shad?"

"Not that I know of, though I've heard it whispered by some that a good shaking of my family tree would uncover a rogue or two."

"What are you looking for?"

"Dr. White. There's no point in us wasting time. We'd best be about seeing to our passage to Panama City over on the west coast." Morgan grabbed a passing man by the arm. "Do you know where we can find Dr. White from the *Eagle?*"

"Nobody from the *Eagle*'s seen hide nor hair of him since we landed," the man answered. "He seems to have vanished into thin air."

Morgan frowned, his right hand coming to rest on the butt of his .31, which protruded from his waistband. "Me and my friend here, we each paid him twenty-five dollars to arrange for us to get from here to Panama City."

"You're not the only ones who did. Most of us who were on the *Eagle* did."

"You're looking for Dr. White?" inquired a bearded man who happened to be passing and who had apparently overheard the conversation between Morgan and the other passenger from the *Eagle.* "I'm afraid, gentlemen, you are out of luck. I arrived here over a month ago and have been here ever since, recovering from isthmus fever, which laid me low and which still keeps me from enjoying my lot in life. On my ship there was also a man who called himself Dr. White. I have learned during my sojourn on these desolate shores that these apparently ubiquitous Dr. Whites are nothing but crooks in collusion with steamship agents in New York, bent on separating emigrants from their cash as fast as ever they can. Upon arrival here in Chagres the Dr. Whites of our evil world vanish like smoke on a windy day."

Morgan swore.

"Did your Dr. White sell you quinine powders?" the man asked.

"He sold me some," Jamieson replied as Morgan shook his head. "I bought twelve packets of quinine powder from the *Eagle*'s Dr. White for two dollars apiece. He said they'd keep me from getting the fever."

The man laughed and then, sobering, said, "I'm sorry. I shouldn't laugh at your plight. It was, after all, once mine. I, too, bought packets of quinine powder from the Dr. White aboard my ship, but I nevertheless wound up with a bad case of isthmus fever because the contents of the packets I bought contained, I discovered to my chagrin, sugar, not quinine."

"I'll kill him!" Jamieson exclaimed, his fingers forming fists. "If I ever see that son of a bitch who called himself Dr. White again, I'll rip him apart with my bare hands!"

"We're obliged to you for the information," Morgan told the man. "Come on, Cass."

"Come on where?"

"It looks like it's up to us to get ourselves from here to the west coast. Let's set about doing just that, what do you say?" Morgan, carrying his carpetbag, headed for the spot where a cluster of Panamanian Indians, naked except for their wide-brimmed hats, stood beside their dugouts. Jamieson, luggage in hand, followed at his heels.

They halted at the water's edge and stood listening to the bargaining that was taking place among a number of California-bound men and several stolid Indians who stood leaning in silence on poles and paddles.

"Twenty American dollars to Gorgona!" shouted a man, waving folding money in the face of one of the boatmen.

The Indian merely shrugged.

"Don't any of you blasted buggers speak English?" bellowed the frustrated traveler as he wiped a sheen of sweat from his forehead with the back of his hand.

No response from any of the Indians.

"Twenty-five dollars!" the man offered and again met with no response from the silently staring Indians.

"Thirty!" the man shouted.

The Indian nearest him broke into a broad grin and gleefully pointed with his pole to one of the dugouts. "You come. Give money. We go."

"Well I'll be damned!" the successful bidder for the boatman's services exclaimed as he handed thirty dollars to the Indian. "Ain't it a miracle how top dollar will teach these boys to speak the King's English?" He turned to gather up his luggage and provisions, and as he did so he let out an angry bellow. "The buggers," he shouted. "They've made off with all my worldly possessions!" He went running up on the beach in search of the thieves, causing the Indians to snicker and whisper among themselves.

"What's the going rate?" Morgan asked one of the men in the crowd on the beach.

"Used to be, I'm told," the man replied, "these here bungos—that's what the natives call them, bungos—would take you as far as Gorgona for ten dollars. Maybe a little less. But these boys have heard about what's happening in California. Oh, it's wise they've grown now and we're the unlucky sots what has to pay for their newfound wisdom. They've upped their prices considerable."

"How high?" Morgan asked.

"You could maybe get a bungo and a pair of boatmen to take you as far as Gorgona for twenty or so dollars these days. Maybe a mite more."

"How far is Gorgona from Panama City?" Jamieson asked.

"About twenty miles."

"How do we get from Gorgona to Panama?"

"On foot. Or on mules they've got there for hire, it's said."

"Well, the first thing facing us," Morgan mused, "is to get ourselves a bungo and the men to power it."

"Try getting one for twenty," the man standing beside him advised. "You might get lucky and the boatman'll go for it. Unless some of these other fellows in their unseemly eagerness to become millionaires out in California don't outbid you."

"Offering twenty dollars sounds to me like a waste of time," Jamieson declared. "Fifty dollars!" he called out and was immediately pounced upon by three bungo boatmen, each of whom began to drag him toward three widely separated dugouts drawn up on the beach, practically pulling him apart in the violent process.

Morgan lunged forward and managed to end the miniature melee. "Twenty dollars," he offered.

"Fifty," shot back one of the Indians as the other two turned away to bargain with other men on the beach.

Morgan shook his head. He pointed to Jamieson and then to himself. "Two men only." He pointed to his carpetbag and Jamieson's suitcase. "Not heavy load."

"Forty-five dollars!" the Indian countered.

"You make fast trip," Morgan persisted. "Come back here. Make other trip. Get forty, fifty dollars in same time it take you to haul many men and goods one time to Gorgona."

The Indian frowned, thought a moment. "Twenty-five dollar?"

Morgan hesitated. He glanced at Jamieson, who nodded. The Indian whistled, and another Indian materialized out of the crowd on the beach and climbed into a dugout.

When both Morgan and Jamieson were seated beside their luggage in the small craft, the boatman with whom Morgan had bargained held out his hand. "Pay bungo boys now."

Morgan and Jamieson split the fee between

them, and Morgan handed the man twenty-five dollars. A moment later they were being poled away from the beach and skimming across the dark surface of the Chagres River on their way to the west coast.

As they left the harbor and the village behind them, they moved into a world the like of which Morgan had never before seen. He found himself marveling at the sight of the lush green canopy of trees whose branches met and intertwined above the winding path of the river. In the emerald world of those leafy branches, slashes of color abounded, now visible, now hidden from sight—toucans and parrots, pigeons and wild turkeys. Morgan and the others were at times forced to duck to avoid becoming entangled in the hanging vines that reached hundreds of feet in length. Down them clambered small monkeys screeching all the way and baring their bright white teeth at the invaders of their jungle domain.

"How long will it take us to get to Gorgona?" Jamieson asked the man who was poling the bungo.

"Four days, mebbe so five."

Jamieson slapped at the swarm of mosquitoes surrounding him and grimaced at the bloody mush his blow had left on his face. He wiped it away and flicked it from his fingers into the water, remarking to Morgan as he did so, "I always thought of hell as being as red as a hot poker. Now I know it's really green."

Morgan grinned and gazed up at the land that sloped away above banks five feet high, on which grazed goats and several head of cattle. He coughed as the boat glided into a stretch of the river from which rose thick vapors that almost hid the river's banks from view as it swirled about the boat and the men in it.

As the day wore on and the sun rose higher in the sky, the jungle became a fetid swamp. Sweat poured down Morgan's face and was squeezed by the oppressive heat from every pore in his baked body. His clothes quickly became wet with sweat and they clung damply to him, seeming to weigh him down. But dazzled as he was by the sights and sounds of the jungle around him, he gave little thought to his discomfort. Instead he found himself thinking, as he stared up at the giant fronds of a fern gently swaying in the humid breeze wafting over the water, of the homeplace he had left where the nearest thing he had ever seen to what he was now witnessing was the fertile miracle of each summer's young green corn as it sprouted in the fields and buried the land beneath its bright green bounty.

He thought of New England winters, of sleds and frozen ponds to skate on, of pumps that would give no water while they wore a cap of ice like a king's crystal crown. No snow, he thought. Not here, not ever. Another marvel, another wonder in a world that seemed inundated with them.

"Jesus Christ!" Jamieson exclaimed, and Morgan turned to face him and then looked in the direction he was pointing.

"Alligators," Jamieson whispered as he stared in awe at the dark snouts rising up out of the dark morass that was the river. "It most certainly wouldn't do to take a tumble overboard. Not here, it wouldn't. A man who did would make a fast meal for those ugly beasts." His right hand closed on the side of the dugout, and his knuckles turned white as he gripped it firmly.

That night they made camp and a fire on the riverbank. They ate a meal made from the provisions they had bought at Chagres while waiting for "Dr. White" to put in an appearance.

"I get a mouthful of mosquitoes every time I try to take a bite," Jamieson complained.

Morgan bit into the piece of fruit Jamieson had handed him and began to chew. He grimaced and spat.

Jamieson looked up and laughed when he saw what Morgan had done. "Like this," he said, demonstrating how to eat the fruit. "You have to peel it first. You don't eat the skin of bananas."

"That's what this thing's called? Bananas?"

"*A* banana, yes."

Morgan peeled back the yellow skin and bit into the white pulpy fruit. "Not bad," he commented a moment later. "A man just has to know how to go about a thing to get the true benefit of it, I reckon."

"I reckon," Jamieson playfully agreed.

Later, as the fire died down and Morgan tried to sleep, he found that he could not do so because of the ubiquitous mosquitoes that infested the tropical darkness as they fought to feast on any available flesh, including his. In the morning, after a sleepless night, he climbed wearily into the dugout with Jamieson, and the journey up the Chagres continued to a chorus of busily buzzing mosquitoes, squealing monkeys and shrieking birds.

That afternoon they passed a crude cross made with tree branches bound with twine, which stood alone and forlorn above a mounded grave in a small clearing near the bank of the river.

"Some poor devil never made it," Jamieson commented solemnly. "Fever, no doubt." Later that day, when they passed two more similar symbols that marked the end of the journey for two other unknowns, Jamieson said nothing, and Morgan, as he watched the crosses glide past him as the bungo proceeded on its westerly course, thought of the miles that lay ahead of them and fought down the urge to speculate upon what other dangers might be lurking ahead on the path he was and would be following in the future.

On the third morning following their departure from Chagres, Morgan, who had taken to sleeping with both hands thrust deep into his pockets and a handkerchief strategically tied around his head so that it covered his face, was awakened by a foot nudging him in the ribs. He pulled the handkerchief aside and blinked up at the naked Indian who stood looking down at him. "Time to go?" he asked, resisting the impulse to seize the Indian's ankle and twist it hard enough to make the man's offending foot fall off. As he started to rise, the Indian grunted and muttered, "No go."

Jamieson, lying on the ground next to Morgan, stirred and sat up. "What's wrong, Shad? What does he mean, 'no go'?"

The Indian, as if in response to Jamieson's question, pointed upriver with the paddle he held in his hand. "You give more money, we go. You no give more money"—he pointed in the direction from which they had come—"bungo boys go that way. You walk Gorgona."

"Listen, mister," Morgan said angrily as he got to his feet, "we already paid you for our passage, so what kind of stunt is this you're trying to pull now?"

The Indian held out his hand.

Morgan ignored it. "I'll be damned if I'll—"

"Oh, pay the bastard what he wants, Shad," Jamieson interrupted. "Let's pay the robbers and get on with it."

"—pay you another single cent," Morgan concluded, ignoring Jamieson.

"You walk Gorgona," said the Indian and turned to go, heading for the bungo that was beached on the river not far away.

Morgan muttered something under his breath. "Cass, my pa used to say that a man's the only animal in the whole wide world that can be skinned more'n once. I reckon he was right. First it was that fellow who called himself Dr. White—no, the first one to try skinning the both of us was that steamship agent back in New York City. Now these two boys figure on fleecing us or else leaving us here to hoof it the rest of the way through this jungle to Gorgona. Well, I'm not having any of it."

"But what can we do about it except pay up? I don't relish the idea of trying to walk to Gorgona. Not with all the snakes and centipedes and scorpions we've seen since we left Chagres. Maybe it wasn't fever that killed whoever it is that's lying buried in those three graves we saw today. Maybe it was snakes."

"Hold on, you!" Morgan yelled and went after the two Indians. They were both climbing into their bungo when Morgan reached them. He seized the one who had demanded the additional payment by the shoulder.

The man responded with a loud grunt and swung the paddle in his hand, which struck Morgan and knocked him to the ground.

"Just you two take it easy," Morgan bellowed when he had caught his breath and gotten to his feet. "I want to talk—"

Again the paddle whirled through the air. This time it cracked against Morgan's ribs, sending pain spearing through his chest. As fury rose red within him, he grabbed the paddle with both hands and ripped it out of the Indian's hands. After throwing it to the ground and before the startled man could speak or move so much as a muscle, Morgan's right fist went flying into the man's face. The roundhouse right knocked the Indian backward. He collided with his companion, who pushed him aside and sprang at Morgan.

But Morgan was ready for him. He delivered a hard left uppercut that landed on the man's lower jaw and snapped his head backward, sending his straw hat flying from his head.

"Look out, Shad!"

Jamieson's warning was unnecessary, because Morgan had already seen the Indian he had struck first pick up a fallen tree branch and lunge at him. He stepped adroitly out of his attacker's way and thrust out one booted foot, tripping the man.

Jamieson came running, a large rock gripped tightly in his right hand. As both Indians went for Morgan, Jamieson brought the rock down on the naked shoulder of one of the two Indians, tearing flesh and drawing blood. The blow caused the man to cry out in pain and stumble awkwardly to one side. While the man was still off balance, Jamieson moved in on him, gave him a shove and sent him tumbling head over heels down the bank and into the vaporous waters of the river, where he quickly disappeared from sight.

Morgan thrust up his left arm to ward off a blow the other Indian tried to deliver and then threw a savage right jab that smashed into his attacker's gut, doubling him over and dropping him to his knees. He raised both fists, stepped back and said to the Indian, "Get in the bungo. We're moving out."

At that moment the other Indian surfaced in the murky river and let out a scream as an alligator suddenly appeared and seized his legs in its jaws. He began to flail his arms, stirring up a muddy froth on the surface of the water. Morgan stared transfixed, as did the Indian on his knees in front of him, at the man in the water who fell forward, his scream dying as his head went underwater again.

Morgan ran to the water's edge, drawing his revolver from his waistband as he went. But when he reached the water's edge he didn't fire, afraid that if he did, he might hit the Indian who was thrashing about wildly in the jaws of the alligator. He thrust his gun back into his waistband, bent and pulled from his right boot the knife he had taken from the man named Trask during their fistfight in New York City. He waded into the water but had not gone more than a few steps when he found himself immobilized, his boots mired in the mud of the river bottom. The knife remained useless in his hand because its intended target, the alligator, was a good four feet away. He struggled but failed to free himself from the mud.

As another gnarled snout rose out of the water not far from where Morgan stood stuck in the sucking mud and both baleful eyes of a second alligator glared at him, Jamieson ran to the riverbank and thrust out a hand to Morgan. At the same instant the first alligator opened its jaws, and the momentarily freed and badly injured Indian scrambled through the water that was red with his own blood in a desperate effort to reach the safety of the bank.

Morgan managed to pull one foot free of the mud. He returned his knife to his boot and took a step toward the Indian, his hands outthrust to help the man. The Indian reached for his hands, but a moment before he would have clasped them in his own, Morgan saw what seemed to be a tree dart past him on the right side and slam into the man's chest. The Indian toppled over backward into the water, and a horrified Morgan shuddered as both alligators quickly converged on the fallen man, dragging him under the water and out of sight.

Morgan felt a hand land on his shoulder and he was about to turn, instinctively ready to defend himself, when he heard Jamieson say, "I'll pull and together we'll get you out of there." Moments later Morgan was lying on his back on the riverbank, panting from the effort to get out of the river, while Jamieson stood with the tree branch he had used to strike the Indian who had been struggling to escape from the alligator and stared down at the water that was alive with rapidly spreading ripples.

"Is he—" Morgan began.

"Gone," Jamieson said and turned to look down at Morgan. "You all right?"

Morgan managed a feeble nod. "I thought there for a minute I might be a goner."

"I'm glad you weren't."

"I'm obliged to you for what you did for me, Cass."

Jamieson shrugged.

Morgan stared up at him. He started to ask the ugly question that was on his mind, but the words would not come to him.

Jamieson, still staring down at him and perhaps sensing what was on Morgan's mind, shrugged again. "If that savage had gotten a hand on you, Shad, he would have dragged you down with him and you'd both have fed the alligators as he's just done."

He's right, Morgan thought. I know he is. But—

"Don't look so down in the dumps, Shad. You're safe and in one piece. That's the important thing. And he was only an Indian, after all."

*Only an Indian, after all.*

The words chilled Morgan despite the blistering heat of the jungle sun. So did the faint smile on Jamieson's face.

"It looks like the other Indian has run off on us, Shad," Jamieson said as he bent and picked up the abandoned pole and paddle. He held them out in front of him and, still smiling, asked, "Do you want to pole or paddle?"

They arrived at the village of Gorgona on the Chagres River two days later, during a drenching downpour that almost blinded them with its relentless fury. Beaching the bungo, they unloaded what was left of their provisions along with their luggage and made their way to the nearest hut. Entering it, they found a young man and two women seated inside, each of them wearing only strings of beads.

"Mules?" queried Jamieson. "Three mules how much?"

The man smiled, slapped one of the two

women on her ample rump and said something in their language to her that caused her to scurry out of the hut. Turning back to Morgan and Jamieson, he held up ten fingers once, twice, thrice.

"Thirty dollars!" Jamieson exclaimed. "That's highway robbery!" But he nevertheless withdrew his purse from his pocket, and when Morgan had handed him fifteen dollars, he gave the money to the smiling Indian, who tucked it under a blanket lying on the ground at his feet.

The Indian beckoned, and Morgan and Jamieson followed him outside, where they found the woman who had earlier left the hut driving three mules toward them through the driving rain. Both men set about loading their provisions and luggage on the back of one of the mules and lashing the bags and boxes in place. When they had completed their task, Jamieson looked at Morgan and said, "How the hell do you get aboard one of these damned donkeys, do you know?"

Morgan grinned and was about to demonstrate the technique he had learned as a boy on the homeplace when a bedraggled white man came lurching out of the jungle. His long blond hair was plastered to his narrow forehead. His dark brown eyes looked alternately angry and desperate. His bony body was covered with mud, his clothes were torn in places, he was hatless, and one of his shoes was missing.

"Mule!" he muttered, the sound of the word almost washed away by the rain.

The Indian spoke to the woman who had brought the three mules, and she turned and ran away through the rain, disappearing around the side of the hut.

"You boys just arrived, did you?" the new-comer asked in a weary voice. When he received a nod from Morgan in reply, he continued. "It's but twenty miles from here to the city of Panama, but by golly, I'm beginning to think I never will make it. I've tried twice. First time on foot. I couldn't even get up to the summit of the mountain that stands between here and Panama. The second time my mule went down the side of the mountain, taking me with him. He's dead. My name's Tyler Conrad."

Morgan and then Jamieson shook Conrad's outstretched hand and introduced themselves.

"Call me Ty," Conrad said. "Tyler always did sound to me like the name of some slick politician."

The woman returned with a fourth mule, and Conrad paid her for it with a gold eagle he took from a drawstringed leather pouch.

"I hope you don't mind if I tag along with you fellows," he said. "Maybe if I do I'll have better luck than the last two times I tried making it on my own."

"What about your gear?" Morgan asked him.

"Lost it all along with my mule. Down a deep gorge. I'm just glad I had my poke in my pocket."

Morgan boarded his mule and so did Conrad. When Jamieson, on his third attempt, was up on his mount, the three men moved out, Morgan leading the pack mule by the woven grass rope the Indian woman had placed around its neck.

The rain continued to try to drown the three travelers as they began their journey up the mountain. They followed an almost invisible trail as they made their way up steep slopes, down into almost impassably narrow ravines and through dense jungle vegetation that whipped their faces and seemed determined to claw the clothes from their bodies and the hats from their heads.

Several times Morgan shifted position on his mule, but no matter how he moved, the sharp spine of the scrawny animal seemed about to split him in half.

The rain stopped in mid-afternoon, and the

sky cleared almost instantly. Down upon the three men then beat the brassy beams of the tropical sun, while all around them vapors rose from the dripping foliage and the muddy ground. They passed dead mules, which lay swollen and stinking on the path, while above the carcasses vultures winged in endless circles. An hour before sundown they passed two Indians carrying a litter suspended from a long pole in which lay a white man with his eyes closed and his arms dangling to trail along the ground.

"Isthmus fever," Conrad commented laconically as they left the litter bearers and their burden behind. "Men have been dying like flies from it."

When the sun disappeared, they discussed the matter, and despite the discomforts of the journey, they agreed to continue through the night without stopping. Several hours later, they crested the mountain and started the descent, which in some ways proved to be worse than the ascent. The mules, generally surefooted, nevertheless did slip on occasion, and once Conrad was pitched to the soggy ground from which he rose cursing and vowing that "This time I damn well will make it. The third time's the charm."

And make it they did. At dawn the next morning, they arrived in the City of Panama and found it beautiful, with the sun making lovely the architecture of the old Spanish houses and bringing even greater brilliance to the lush gardens that were bursting with gaudy tropical flowers. They crossed an old stone bridge with tall arches, and Morgan found himself marveling at the sight of a majestic cathedral that stood like some relic of the Old World somehow magically transported here to the new one.

"We can maybe get us a room at one of the *pensiones* here," Conrad said. "I heard from a man back in Chagres who was heading home from the gold fields that the rooms were clean and not too dear."

Morgan and the others began to make the rounds of the *pensiones* but soon learned from a toothless old man who spoke a confusing mixture of Spanish, English and an African dialect that there were no rooms to be had anywhere because the city was overcrowded with men awaiting the arrival of a ship bound for San Francisco.

"We've been sleeping outdoors since we left Chagres," Morgan pointed out to Jamieson. "I reckon we can keep on doing so."

"I want a bath," Conrad said. "How about you boys?"

Morgan and Jamieson followed him to the

beach, where, after they found a secluded spot, all three men stripped and proceeded to bathe in the warm water, scrubbing their dirty bodies with sand scooped from the ocean floor. Afterward they washed their clothes in the salty water and spread them on the beach to dry.

That night they ate a meal of Spanish food in a small candlelit restaurant in the plaza. During it, Jamieson complained that the food was too heavily spiced to suit his taste. "Look how it makes me sweat," he pointed out as he wiped his face with a handkerchief.

By the time they had finished their meal and bedded down beside the fountain in the plaza for the night, Jamieson was sweating profusely.

The next morning Morgan awoke to the sound of someone moaning. He sat up and saw Jamieson, who was lying next to him, tossing and turning. And still sweating. "You all right, Cass?" Bad dream, he thought. Nightmare, maybe, and no wonder after what we've been through. "Cass?"

He received a mumbled, incoherent response.

Conrad, on Morgan's left, awoke and, blinking, sat up. He yawned and then, looking down at Jamieson, asked, "What's wrong with him?" Without waiting for an answer, he sucked in his breath and whispered, "Isthmus fever."

Morgan glanced at him. "You think so?"

Conrad nodded and moved away. "I've seen it before. Look—he's got the shakes."

Morgan looked back at Jamieson and noticed for the first time that the man was trembling. He put a hand on Jamieson's shoulder and gently shook him.

Jamieson's eyes opened. So did his lips, from which issued in a rapid flow words Morgan could not understand. Then, "I'll show you! You just see if I don't!"

"Cass?" Morgan squeezed Jamieson's shoulder.

"You want some well-meant advice, Shad?" Conrad asked nervously, moving even farther away. "Leave him be. The fever—some men say it's catching, though nobody really knows for sure, or even what causes it."

"What'd you say, mister?" barked a man sitting nearby with his back braced against the fountain. "Did you say fever?"

"He's got himself a case of it," Conrad answered, nodding and pointing at Jamieson.

The other men in the area, joined by Conrad, moved quickly away, the word *fever* a fearful whisper on all their lips. Morgan quickly found himself alone with Jamieson. He pulled the man's handkerchief from his pocket, soaked it in the water of the fountain, and wiped Jamieson's face. But the sweat continued to ooze out of Jamieson's pores, and his face was almost immediately slick once again. Morgan got up and, gripping Jamieson under the arms, dragged him out of the sun and into a patch of shade on the far side of the fountain.

"You never had any use for me," Jamieson whispered weakly.

"That's not true, Cass," Morgan countered. "You and me, we're friends."

"Ever since I was born . . ." Jamieson's voice faded away. Then, more strongly, he said, "No decent father would have treated his son the way you treated me. You treated me like dirt. I was never good enough to suit you. Never fast enough in a foot race. Never strong enough. Not clever. *According to you.*"

Morgan realized that Cass was talking feverishly to his father, not to him.

"—wouldn't let me be me," he mumbled. "You *wouldn't!* A lawyer. That's what I had to be. Because *you* decided I should be one!" Jamieson abruptly sat up, his eyes wild, his right arm outstretched, an indicting index finger pointing at nothing as he screamed, "I'll *not* be a lawyer. *Not* be like you. But I *will* be rich.

You'll see! One way or another, I'll come home rich and then—and then—"

"Lie down, Cass," Morgan urged as huge tears began to course down Jamieson's quivering cheeks. "Take it easy, Cass, do."

"And then," Jamieson continued, unmindful or unaware of Morgan's soothing words, "maybe —just maybe—*you'll love me.*" He collapsed into Morgan's arms, sobs racking his hot body.

Morgan laid him down in the shade and again bathed his face. He hesitated a moment and then rose and ran across the plaza to a general store, where he bought a blanket. When he returned he wrapped Jamieson in it, and throughout the rest of the day, during which he fed him soup he bought from the restaurant at which they had dined the night before, he patiently replaced the blanket every time Jamieson threw it off, protesting that he was too hot.

During the next two days, in Jamieson's occasional moments of lucidity, he complained of pains in his back and legs. He avoided the light because, he said, it hurt his eyes. He experienced fits of violent vomiting that left him drained. During that time, Morgan left his side only long enough to relieve himself or to buy food for himself and Jamieson. At the end of the second day, he found that Jamieson's temperature seemed to have returned to normal. But the following morning Jamieson was once again feverish, and his skin began to turn yellow. Morgan continued to tend to him.

When Conrad reappeared on the fourth day after the onset of Jamieson's illness, he told Morgan that he had heard that a Pacific Mail steamer was due to dock at Panama within the next few days. "You'd best buy your ticket now, Shad," he advised. "They've only got just so much room for fellows like us, seeing as how they're pretty well loaded down, I'm told, with men who booked passage around Cape Horn from the States."

"How much is the fare?"

"Two hundred."

Morgan counted out two hundred dollars of his own and then took two hundred from Jamieson's purse and handed the total amount to Conrad. "I'd be obliged to you, Ty, if you'd secure two tickets for me and Cass."

Conrad glanced sharply at Morgan. "You're sticking by him?" When Morgan nodded, Conrad asked, "You're not sick, are you?"

"Nope."

"Good. I'll just hop on over to the Pacific Mail office and be back with your tickets in two shakes of a mule's tail."

# FOUR

Bedlam came to the City of Panama with the arrival, three days later, of the Pacific Mail's steamer *Cape Horn.*

Morgan stood in the plaza with Conrad and a still-jaundiced but no longer feverish Jamieson at his side, and they watched the mob of men who were shouting and pounding on the doors and windows of the Pacific Mail office.

"That's Agent Rheiner," Conrad stated, pointing to the harried man who emerged from the building. "The one I bought our tickets from. He looks like he's about to expire."

Rheiner did. His small dark eyes darted here and there among the crowd as if trying to find some resting place where they would be welcome. Finding none, they continued to flit and flicker about as he waved his hands above his head and shouted at the top of his voice in an attempt to quiet the crowd so that he could be heard. He finally succeeded and, having done so, drew a deep breath and exclaimed, "I am most sincerely sorry, gentlemen, but facts are facts and they must be faced by us all. There is simply no more room available on the *Cape Horn*. None. I repeat: *none*. I can therefore sell no more tickets."

A lusty roar of protest welled up from the crowd. Men shook their fists at Agent Rheiner, who stiffened and stepped backward, apparently seeking the refuge of his office in the building behind him.

"Deck space!" someone in the crowd yelled. "Sell us deck space!"

"I have already sold over two dozen such tickets," Rheiner declared. "Captain Lansing insists that he will take no more deck passengers."

Conrad pulled out his ticket, glanced at it, and then thrust it back in his pocket. He shrugged. "Deck space was the best I could get for us," he stated somewhat apologetically. "We'll be at the mercy of the wind and rain out there on that ship's deck. Them and the full moon, which I've heard it said drives some men mad."

"Deck space'll be fine," Morgan told him. "It'll be a far sight better than being left here on the beach, though Panama City is, to tell the truth about it, a pretty place."

"It's hard to believe that California will be

any better," Jamieson mused. "That it *could* be any better than this."

"Ah, but you can rest assured that it is, my bucko!" roared Conrad, beaming jovially. "There's no gold *here*, but in California. . . ." He rolled his eyes and licked his lips.

"Let's draw and quarter Rheiner!" yelled a man in the crowd.

"String him up to the nearest tree!" urged another man.

As the crowd, like some amorphous organism propelled by the power of frustration and rage, surged forward, Agent Rheiner turned and fled inside the building. He slammed and bolted the door behind himself and then hung a sign in the window that read: CLOSED.

"Everybody's in a hurry to get to the gold fields," Jamieson said softly. "Those fellows can't bear to wait, it seems, for the next ship. Certainly not for the one after that."

"Everybody's afraid that the gold will all be gone by the time they get to California," Conrad said. "Those latecomers over there who shall, it appears, remain ticketless for a time, are no different from any of the rest of us. If I had no ticket, I'd be right up there in the front of that crowd, howling and yelling and doing my dance while I tried my damnedest to get a ticket to travel to El Dorado."

"If the Pacific Mail agent had more tickets for sale," Jamieson mused thoughtfully as if he were talking to himself, "I've not the least doubt that he could get top dollar for them."

"'Tis true, Cass," Conrad said, nodding agreement.

"Looking at the matter through the eyes of those latecomers to Panama City," Morgan said, "a ticket to California on anything that floats would right now be worth its weight—a whole lot more than that, I reckon—in gold." He grinned.

Jamieson didn't. He pulled his ticket from his pocket and looked at it. Then he looked up at the crowd that was still surging like an angry sea in front of the Pacific Mail building.

"Where are you headed?" Morgan asked him as Jamieson began to move slowly away.

Jamieson stopped, looked back. "One of the ways to get rich, my friends, is to spot an opportunity to make money and then seize that opportunity. That is precisely what I intend to do."

"I don't follow you, Cass," Morgan said.

Jamieson held his ticket aloft. "I paid two

hundred dollars for this ticket. I can't help wondering just how much I can sell it for."

"Sell it?" Conrad piped incredulously.

"What for would you want to do a crazy thing like that, Cass?" Morgan asked, genuinely puzzled.

"What for? Why to make money, that's why."

"Let me get this straight," Morgan said. "You're fixing to sell your ticket—"

"To the highest bidder, yes, I am."

"And do what then?" a wide-eyed Conrad asked. "Stay here? Head back home?"

"There will be another ship," Jamieson stated confidently. "Maybe today. Maybe tomorrow. Or the day after that. And I'll be on it. I do hate leaving you boys with no one to look after you, but—" he smiled at his companions—"I can't pass up this opportunity."

Jamieson turned and headed for the crowd. Moments later, he was in the midst of it and shouting at the top of his voice that he had a ticket on the *Cape Horn* for sale. "What's it worth to you, gentlemen?"

The response to his question was overwhelming. Men bellowed their bids in loud voices. *Two hundred. Three hundred. Three hundred and ten. Three hundred and fifty. Five hundred.*

When the bidding ended minutes later, Jamieson had sold his ticket to a jubilant emigrant for one thousand two hundred and twenty dollars.

He returned to Morgan and Conrad, counting his money and beaming. "It may be awhile, my friends, before I can join you in California. It has just occurred to me that if I am one of the first to buy a ticket on the next ship due to dock here, I can repeat the process I just went through and be rich by the time I get to the gold fields, which would not make me an unhappy man. In fact," he continued after a thoughtful moment, "why buy just one ticket? Why not buy several? Perhaps a dozen?"

"They'll catch on to your scheme," Morgan cautioned. "Agent Rheiner'll likely put a stop to it."

"By the time he does—if he does," a smiling Jamieson said, "I'll have made my money and be ready, I suspect, for a change of scene."

"All aboard!" yelled a male voice from the beach.

"Where will I be liable to find you, Morgan, once I get to California?" Jamieson asked, his mien suddenly serious.

"I don't rightly know how to answer that, Cass," Morgan replied. "California's such a big place—but I'll tell you this. I heard, when I was still back East, that the American River was a good place to hunt for gold. You might find me someplace along the river."

"I hope I do," Jamieson said as he shook hands with Morgan. "Thanks for everything you've done for me, my good friend. I won't forget it. And I hope to see you again one of these days. Good luck to you. The same to you, Ty."

Ty shook hands with Jamieson, and then he and Morgan hurried, caught up in the swarm of ticket holders, down to the water's edge, where boats waited to take the emigrants out to the *Cape Horn* riding at anchor in the harbor.

"I'll be in San Francisco soon
  And there I'll look around,
  And when I see the gold lumps there
  I'll pick them off the ground.
  I'll scrape the mountains clean, my boys,
  I'll drain the rivers dry,
  A pocket full of rocks bring home,
  So brothers, don't you cry."

Morgan sat on the deck of the steamer in the darkness and listened to the convivial noise being made by some nearby men as they sang the hopeful words, which were set to the tune of Stephen Foster's popular song "O Susanna."

But despite the sound of the singing, he could still hear the ominous series of wet *plups* made by shrouded bodies that were being dumped into the sea by some of the *Cape Horn* deckhands. The grim ritual of disposing of those men who had died of isthmus fever aboard the ship continued. So did the singing.

> "The pilot bread was in my mouth,
> The gold dust in my eye,
> But though I'm going far away—
> Dear brothers, don't you cry."

*Plup. Plup-plup.*

Morgan looked away from the deckhands as they lifted and heaved over the rail the lifeless body of another man bereft of both dreams and life, a man who would never see not only the fabled land of California but that night's stars or the coming morning's rising sun.

"We're almost there, Shad," Conrad said as he appeared like a specter out of the shadows shed by the deckhouse.

"And glad it is I am that we are," Morgan responded, his eyes on the starlit California coastline gliding dimly past in the distance. "It seems to me I've been on my way to California forever."

"It's the longing that makes it seem that way.

The heartfelt longing to finally be there, to find that fortune and then turn your face away from a strange land and start back home again." Conrad paused. "You don't think it's a trick, do you, Shad?"

"A trick? What are you talking about, Ty?"

"I've heard talk among the men on board. They say, some of them do, that maybe there's been no gold strike in California a'tall. They think somebody might be spreading stories to get people to come all the way out here from the States to settle the land. Do you think that's possible?"

"It's possible enough; sure it is. But I truly hope it's no trick. I'm counting on finding me my share of that gold."

"I know what you mean. I've hardly been able to think of anything else but gold since I started out. That's all that's talked about. I even have dreamed about it." A wry smile appeared on Conrad's face as he sat down on the deck next to Morgan. "I'll tell you something, Shad. Our friend Cass Jamieson—now there's a fellow that will get rich whether or not there's so much as a speck of gold to be found in California. Take that stunt he pulled back there before we left Panama Bay. What did you think of that, Shad?"

"You mean the way he sold his ticket for a tidy profit?"

Conrad nodded.

"Well, I guess you've got to give him credit. He's nothing if not enterprising. I confess selling my ticket to fatten my purse never even entered my mind. I guess that's what comes of having a college education."

"Jamieson has himself one?"

"He told me he went to Harvard University to see about becoming a lawyer, only he left on account of he, like the rest of us, got the gleam of gold in his eye."

"It seemed to me to be a kind of slippery way he went about the thing he did. Even slicker was his idea about going into the business of buying up steamer tickets and selling them at a profit to men back there on the beach without one."

"Cass took a gamble and it paid off, Ty. I reckon we can't fault him for that. He might get to California too late to find any gold for himself. But maybe he figured a bird in his hand in Panama was worth two out in the California bush."

But something about what Jamieson had done rankled in Morgan's mind, although he didn't know exactly what it was that was bothering him. Maybe you're jealous of old Cass, he speculated. Maybe you wish it was you who'd thought up that scheme of his. But he knew, after a probing moment of careful thought, that such was not the case. No, he thought, it's just that what Cass went and did, it smacks of taking advantage of other fellows who're down on their luck, and that's just not the kind of thing I'd feel real comfortable doing.

But wait a minute, he thought. Cass didn't do anything the least little bit wrong. He had something to sell, and by God, there sure were plenty of eager boys back there willing to buy. It was a business transaction, is all. Plain and aboveboard. It wasn't done sneaky the way that steamship agent back in New York City tried in his underhanded way to cheat the two of us out of twenty-five dollars apiece. But, he couldn't help thinking, neither was it altogether unlike what the New York City steamship agent had tried to do. Not when you got right down to the bottom of things, it wasn't.

The sun was almost up, the sky awash with a russet glow, when the *Cape Horn* steamed into San Francisco Bay. Morgan and Conrad stood in the throng that crowded the deck and stared at a dream come true—San Francisco.

"Doesn't look like a whole hell of a lot, does it?" Conrad muttered, frowning.

Morgan stared at the almost treeless coastal hills rising from the sandy beach, where scores of horses and cattle could be seen grazing among the tents and other shelters scattered about. He glanced at Alcatraz Island, and as he did so, great flocks of sea birds, disturbed by the passage of the *Cape Horn,* rose in a thunder of wings into the sky, almost completely obscuring the dawn's bright light.

Morgan's answer to Conrad's question was drowned out by the grating sound of the ship's anchor being dropped and by the even louder sounds of the cheering emigrants on deck, who were waving their hats and wiping the tears from their eyes as they spotted the first of the small boats that were putting out from shore.

"Is it true?" cried one emigrant as the first of the boats reached the *Cape Horn,* and he cried out even louder when he heard, from one of the men in the boat, the reply, "Aye, mate, it's as true as the Holy Word. There's as much as a million dollars a month coming down from the diggings!"

Morgan turned to stare in amazement and joy at a drop-jawed Conrad, who tried to speak to him and couldn't, and instead threw his arms around Morgan and gave him a mighty hug.

"Take it easy, Ty," Morgan, laughing, cautioned. "I declare, man, you've got arms that could squeeze the breath out of a bear."

"Did you hear that, Shad? Did you?" Conrad released Morgan and stepped back, shaking his head in wonderment. "A million dollars a month! Oh, isn't that news to make a man praise the Lord out loud till his lungs burst?"

"I heard," Morgan replied, thinking of his pa, of Gideon and Jonah and Gideon's Nan and wishing they could all be here now to share this moment with him, a moment in which all their fondest dreams were centered and a moment on which all their highest hopes hung.

His thoughts were banished by the fever of activity that broke out aboard the ship as the passengers, who were enthusiastically joined by the ship's sailors despite the pleas of the *Cape Horn*'s captain to remain on board, made arrangements with the boatmen for passage to the shore. He and Conrad, like the other emigrants and the ship's crewmen, who had also been swept up in the gold fever frenzy, soon found themselves in one of the boats. With their luggage, they were quickly rowed ashore, leaving behind them a ship abandoned by its former passengers and all of its crew.

Late that morning, Morgan, with Conrad beside him, walked through the ramshackle settlement that had recently been the Spanish town of Yerba Buena and was now named San Francisco. They wandered the paths that meandered among canvas tents, small adobes, tarpaper shacks, and cloth buildings. They listened to the aimless and high-spirited shooting of the men in the saloons and to the music that came from nowhere and everywhere—fiddle and Jew's harp and, once, a trumpet. Glancing into the interior of one of the saloons, they saw the young and the not-so-young men standing knee-deep in front of the faro tables, and they saw, too, for the very first time, the sacks of shiny gold dust and the glittering gold nuggets that changed hands on the turn of a single card.

The coal oil lamps caught the glint of the gold and made it glisten. Its glow filled Morgan's eyes, and in its tawny splendor he saw many-roomed mansions and flagons of rich red wine, fine clothes and soft beds, doe-eyed women beckoning to him . . .

His vision changed. He saw hired hands—many of them—working the rocky soil of the homeplace while he and his pa and brothers took their ease for a time in the shade of the towering cypress that grew in front of the house. He saw rich harvests and a root cellar bursting with sustenance—enough for a long snowy winter. He saw the smokehouse hung with more slabs of bacon than he could count. A little folded piece of paper that his pa was holding told of the big balance safe in the bank in town. He heard his pa proudly declare that it was he, Shadrach Morgan, they had to thank for it all, because he had bravely gone into the wilderness and returned with a golden fortune that would blind the eyes of a whole world full of wolves to keep them forevermore from the door of the Morgan family's homeplace.

Morgan turned away from the sight of the gold, but it lingered, glowing, in his mind as he and Conrad, by mutual agreement, made their way back down the slopes to San Francisco's lone wharf, where they spent the night out in the open among a number of other men who were also waiting to make their way to the gold fields.

By the light of a candle belonging to one of the other emigrants, Morgan, after borrowing paper and the stub of a pencil from another man, wrote a letter home.

"Dear Pa," he wrote. "I take pen in hand to

tell you that all is well. I am safe and sound in San Francisco. I start out soon on the next part of my journey upriver to Sacramento. There is lots of gold here, Pa. Everybody says so and I saw some for myself tonight. I hope with the good Lord's help to get us our share real soon. How are you all? I miss everybody. Say I said hello to all and don't worry about me. Your son, Shadrach"

In the morning, he mailed his letter at the post office, where Conrad bought a copy of the New York *Tribune* for an exorbitant fifty cents.

"Looky here, Shad," Conrad exclaimed, pointing to the printed sailing schedule of ships bound from New York for San Francisco. "There's nineteen of them. Count 'em. Nineteen due to depart—well, they've departed by now, according to the dates listed here. California soon won't be big enough to hold everybody that's on his way out here. Or *her* way, hopefully. I'd give my eyeteeth for just a look at a woman and never mind if she was plain instead of pretty."

It was not until a week later that they were successful in booking passage on a schooner heading upriver to Sacramento. Upon their arrival there, they bought, from a man vending goods he had brought to town by mule train, provisions, two flat-bottomed tin pans with slanted sides, and cooking utensils. Shouldering their supplies, which they had lashed into two packs, they set out on foot to follow the course of the north fork of the American River as it wound its way east. They walked through the river's verdant flood plain and then made their way through a series of labyrinthine gulches. At the mouth of one of the canyons, they made camp for the night.

Dawn found Morgan standing nearly knee-deep in the river as he began, for the first time, to pan for gold. It wasn't long before his hands were nearly frozen by the icy river water. But he kept at it, swirling dirt in his tilted pan, which he kept below the surface. As he raised it and continued to swirl its contents about, he ignored the silt and stones that washed out of the pan, his eyes hopefully searching the bottom of the pan for a glint of color where gold had settled. He saw none. Flexing his fingers from time to time to keep the blood flowing in them, he kept at it, but he had found no gold by the time Conrad awoke and summoned him to a breakfast that turned out to consist of beans as hard as bullets and coffee blacker than burned molasses and every bit as appetizing.

"Not so good, huh?" Conrad prompted.

"It's no worse than what I came up with last night, Ty. That bread I baked—a bullet couldn't've pierced it—and the pork was as thick with ashes as it was with salt."

"I never thought I'd find myself wishing that my ma had taught me how to cook. I never thought I'd have a need to know how to do woman's work."

After breakfast, both men busied themselves panning for gold. Neither of them found any. But neither of them was discouraged. It was here somewhere, they assured each other several times. Or if not right here, then over there. Or upriver aways. Around the next bend, maybe. All they had to do was stick to it and they'd come up with some. Sooner or later. They were sure of it.

Their hands went numb in the cold river. Their backs threatened to break as they continued bending over the rushing water. Their eyes became bloodshot from staring down at the water that reflected the glare of the rising sun.

That night, as the sun began its descent, they stopped panning and ate, neither man saying much.

The sun was behind a distant ridge when Conrad stood up suddenly and kicked the rock he had been sitting on, dislodging it. "Where the hell is the gold?" he roared. "We freeze our fingers in the river and break our backs leaning over it and we've got not so much as a speck of gold dust to—" He stopped in mid-sentence and stood staring down at the rock he had kicked. Then, in a small voice, "Shad."

Morgan, after forking some beans into his mouth, looked up.

"Shad, look."

Morgan looked and saw what Conrad's trembling index finger was pointing at. His eyes widened. His lips parted and he let out a whoop, dropping his fork and tin plate. He shot to his feet and then bent to pick up the nugget that glowed in the fading light of the sun—the nugget that had been lying hidden in the dirt beneath the rock Conrad's kick had dislodged. He held it up to catch the sun's last light. And then he handed it almost reverently to the dumbstruck Conrad.

"You've done it, Ty," he exulted. "You've found gold!"

"How much you think it might be worth?" Conrad croaked, turning the nugget over and over in his hands.

"That nugget's worth about a hundred dollars."

Morgan turned to stare at the elderly man

leading a mule who had come unheard and unnoticed into their camp and who had just answered Conrad's question.

"A hundred dollars," an obviously impressed Conrad breathed.

"Gold's selling nowadays for two hundred and forty dollars a pound," the old man remarked. "My guess is, like I said, that you can get about a hundred dollars for a nugget that size."

Conrad leapt into the air, kicking his heels together. "A hundred dollars!" he exclaimed gleefully, his right hand tightly clutching his find.

"I'm Emmett Howell," the old man said. "Do you boys mind if I join you? I've got some fresh squirrel meat I don't mind sharing with you."

"Shad Morgan," Morgan said and shook Emmett's hand. "This here's my friend Ty Conrad."

"Glad to meet you both," Emmett said as he retrieved a leather sack from among the provisions lashed to the back of his mule. He opened the sack, and using several sticks he took from the pile Morgan had gathered to feed the fire, proceeded to spear pieces of squirrel meat. He handed one stick to Morgan and one to Conrad.

When all three men were hunkered down together, their portions of meat sizzling over the fire's flames, Emmett asked, "Where'd you find it?"

"Under that rock," Conrad replied. "I kicked the rock and there she was just as big and pretty as any dance hall girl I ever did see."

Emmett looked around the camp. His eyes fell on the two tin pans. "You boys have been placer mining, have you?"

"With nothing to show for it so far," Conrad remarked dolefully as he pocketed his nugget.

"But we've only been at it for part of a day," Morgan pointed out. "We're bound to find some color in time."

Emmett smiled at him. "That's the way to look at it, young feller. Optimistic-like. No use looking on the dark side of things. You do that and you'll end up squinty-eyed." He chortled. "Get it? Trying to see in the dark? Squinty-eyed?"

Morgan smiled as Conrad took his nugget from his pocket and began to fondle it. "You had any luck so far, oldtimer?" he asked.

"Me? Sure I have." Emmett removed his sizzling squirrel meat from the fire and licked his lips as he waited for it to cool.

"*Much* luck?" Conrad prompted.

"Well, sir, I don't rightly know how you measure 'much,' but I guess it's safe to say I've done all right by myself."

"Where?" Morgan asked eagerly.

"Oh, here and there. On the Feather River. On the Stanislaus too. I was up at Dry Diggings for a spell till things pretty much pinched out there."

"Then you must be a rich man," Conrad commented, his gold nugget back in his pocket along with his right hand, which still fondled his find in secret.

"I *was* rich," Emmett stated and took a big bite of the browned squirrel meat. He chewed for a moment and then said, "More than once. But right now I'm poor again." He ate the last of his meat and then fastened another piece to the end of his makeshift spear, which he held over the fire.

"How come?" Morgan inquired. "If you don't mind my asking."

"I'm a cursed man, Shad. I fell in love years ago when I was still back East in Baltimore. I was a lot younger in those days, but my head was turned then and I've never recovered my wits since."

"Women can do that to a man," Conrad solemnly avowed. "They can twist him and turn

him till he doesn't know which way is up anymore."

"That's a true fact, son," Emmett enthusiastically agreed. "And my paramour, she was one
of the worst of the lot at that devilish game. Her
name, boys, was Lady Luck."

"Lady Luck?" Conrad frowned.

"I'm a gambling man," Emmett explained.
"That's my curse. I've found and lost what
amounts to a medium-size fortune since I first
got out here five months ago. But what the hell,
I say." Emmett's face broke into a broad smile.
"I've seen the elephant, as they say, and I've
had myself a helluva good gambling man's time
of it. Besides, why shouldn't I gamble if that's
what makes me happy—sad, though, too, sometimes, I must confess. I mean I'm getting on in
years, and I came out here to have me one final
fling before it's time to have the dirt shoveled
down upon me."

"If I find some color," Morgan said quietly,
"I won't gamble it away. No offense meant,
Emmett. I figure if a man wants to gamble, that
there's his business. What I meant was I got
family counting on me back in the States. I
mean I'm obligated to them. Only one of us
could come out here—there wasn't money

enough for all three of us Morgan boys to— Ah, I talk altogether too much."

"Not at all, boy, not at all," Emmett assured Morgan. "I don't mind hearing a man's story. I've heard plenty of 'em since I been out here, and every one of 'em was interesting. I've heard happy-go-lucky stories and I've heard homesick stories. Which is your kind, Shad?"

"I'm not rightly sure, Emmett. But I can tell you this much. I sure would like to be able to smell some new-mown hay one more time like we used to have back at the homeplace."

"What about you, Ty?" Emmett asked. "What kind of story have you got to tell?"

"Not much of a one. I was born in New York City. I grew up there. My mother—the less said about her and her gentleman friends the better. I never knew my father. I was out on the streets hustling by the time I was ten. When I heard about what was happening here, I made up my mind to come out and try to get rich. I figured I didn't have much of a chance of doing that in the back alleys of New York. There you were lucky to stay alive, never mind about getting rich. That's my story—so far. Like I told you, it's not much of a one. But the best part"— Conrad broke into a grin—"the best part's still to be written, you mark my words." His grin did the impossible—it widened before finally fading.

"Every man's got a story to tell about himself," Emmett remarked, his gaze shifting between Conrad and Morgan. "Out here you run into some pretty wild ones. So far I've met a man who was a zookeeper in Charleston, a pimp from Philadelphia—well, you boys see what I'm getting at. Every one of those men, me very much included same as you two fellows, had one thing in common and that one thing was gold. Or to put it more precise—the dream of finding gold.

"Some of the men I met, though, they had given up on that dream. It drove them for a time but then it just ran out of steam in the face of all the hardships of getting and staying here. You could see it in the eyes of those men. That's where you could see the corpse of their dead dream floating—in their sad or mad eyes. They were heading home, ready to whine for the rest of their natural lives about how the world was lined up against them. But I won't quit. Me, I'll just keep on trying."

"Me too," said Conrad. "I'll get gold one way or another—out of the rivers or the dirt or the mountains—or even the damned trees. It can try hiding from me but I'll stalk it till I've finally run it down."

"Maybe, if your luck holds, Ty," Morgan said, "you'll get rich just by going around connecting the toe of your boot to every California rock you happen to meet."

Conrad's grin returned.

Morgan turned to Emmett and asked, "Where are you headed?"

"Grizzly Flats."

"Grizzly Flats," Morgan repeated. "I never heard of any place by that name."

"That's no doubt, because Grizzly Flats ain't but about two days old," Emmett said. "It's downright amazing how towns—if you can call 'em that—spring up in the diggings. One minute there's nothing around excepting wildcats and raccoons and the next there's a bunch of tents and a herd of men trampling the grass down to dirt. Grizzly Flats's like that, I hear."

"Why are you headed there?" Conrad inquired.

"Heard tell of a rich strike over that way. It's what birthed the town. I thought I'd go have me a look-see."

"Whereabouts is this Grizzly Flats?" Conrad asked.

Emmett pointed to the southeast. "Over that

way from where we're at right now. It's on the American's south fork."

Conrad's eyes shifted, met Morgan's. "Are you thinking what I'm thinking, Shad?"

"Would you mind if we kept you company on your way to Grizzly Flats?" Conrad asked Emmett.

"This here's a free country," Emmett responded jovially. "You're welcome to traipse along with me if you have a mind to. But I feel it's only fair to warn you fellows. There's almost always talk of a big strike farther on somewhere. This one may turn out to be just a flash in the pan. It might have pinched out before the three of us get there. Then again it might not have. A man just never knows. But anyhow, like I said, you're welcome to walk along with me if you want to."

# FIVE

"There she be!" exclaimed an elated Emmett the next day as he crested a rise with Morgan and Conrad flanking him and pointed down at the tableland below them. "Grizzly Flats!"

Morgan stared at the settlement that seemed to be growing before his very eyes. Men were at work on log structures that stood cheek by jowl with canvas tents and hide structures that stretched as far as the eye could see.

"Noisy place for sure," Conrad commented, idly stroking his tawny untrimmed beard.

Morgan was able to make out individual sounds in the cacophony that drifted up the hill. The sound of saws biting into wood. Hammers meeting nails. Mules braying. Gunfire. Someone howling. A hornpipe being played by an unseen musician. Glass shattering.

"She'll be a veritable metropolis by tomorrow morning," Emmett announced in a mildly satirical tone. "Let's go down there and see what news we can turn up."

They did, and within ten minutes they had

been shown cloth pouches and leather bags full of gold dust, flakes, or nuggets. They had heard stories of men who had taken twenty thousand dollars out of the ground in less than a week. They had heard hair-raising tales of grizzly bears roaming the land that had once been theirs alone and roaring their brawny way into tents, terrifying sleeping emigrants. They had been assured that the best place to stake a new claim was on the north bank of the river's south fork, on the south bank of the south fork, west of the flats, east of the flats, downriver, and upriver.

Morgan, slightly overwhelmed by it all into a kind of stupefied speechlessness, turned aside to stare off into the eastern distance at the still snowcapped peaks of the majestic Sierra Nevada mountains.

"You can buy damn near anything you have need of here," a man replied in answer to a question from Conrad about the availability of whiskey.

"See that canvas billowing in the wind over there, for example?" the man continued. "That there's the Good Times saloon."

"I'm inviting you boys to join me in a drink," Conrad suddenly announced when the man he had been talking to left.

Morgan and Emmett followed him to the

building that was, they discovered, an unsteady structure composed of flapping canvas wrapped around four uprights and stretched across a shaky ridgepole.

"Take a look at that," Conrad said with surprise as they entered the saloon, pointing to the bottles of whiskey that were stacked like glassy kindling at one end of the split-log bar that rested on three stout barrels. "All the comforts of home."

"And then some," breathed an obviously awed Emmett as he stopped in his tracks and stood staring slack-jawed at a woman who was sitting at a wooden table on one side of the bar.

Morgan, as he stepped up to the bar with the others, kept his eyes on the woman, who seemed to be studying the drink in her hand with downcast eyes. She's a beauty, he thought to himself. Pretty as new paint on a barn. He noted her large dark eyes, her provocatively arched eyebrows, her full lips. Spanish, he thought. It shows in the dusky color of her skin and that tar-black hair of hers.

Someone was shaking him by the shoulder. He turned. Conrad was asking him if he had fallen asleep. What did he want to drink?

"Whiskey," he answered, the word almost catching in his throat as the woman he was still watching rose and he saw the alluring flare of her hips, her long legs, and their trim ankles, which were visible, like her bare calves, below her short full skirt.

"Let's drink up," Conrad urged as the bartender placed a bottle and three glasses on the bar. "To success."

"To success," Morgan echoed absently, his eyes still on the woman, who turned in his direction.

And then the sound of voices in the saloon, the shouting of several men outside it, and all the other raucous sounds of the rapidly growing Grizzly Flats faded from Morgan's consciousness and he heard only silence as the woman walked toward him, one hand on a hip, the other tossing back her silken black hair.

"Hello," she said as she stopped next to Morgan. Her voice was husky but not harsh. In fact, Morgan found it melodious.

"Ma'am," he said, touching the brim of his hat to her.

"Well, now," Conrad exclaimed, his eyebrows rising in mock surprise. "What have we here?"

"My name's Shad Morgan, ma'am. What do they call you?"

The woman's eyes darkened for a moment, but then, brightly, she replied, "Maria."

"That's a real pretty name," Morgan told her.

"But not nearly as pretty as the little lady herself," Conrad declared. He stepped around Morgan and put an arm around Maria's waist. "What are you doing here in Grizzly Flats?" he asked her.

She shook herself free of him, her eyes still on Morgan. "You will buy me a drink?"

"Sure," Morgan answered. "Sure, I'll buy you a drink. What'll you have?"

"Brandy," Maria told the man behind the bar. When she had a filled glass in her hand, she gave Morgan a small smile and took a sip from it. *"Gracias."*

"One dollar," the barkeep said to Morgan, who promptly paid him.

Conrad reached out and took Maria's drink from her hand. He took a sip, set the glass down on the bar, and then snatched Morgan's money from the barkeep's hand. "I guess I've got the answer to my question now," he said darkly.

"What question?" Morgan, puzzled, asked him.

"I asked the lady before what she was doing here in Grizzly Flats. Well, what she's doing here is hustling farm boys like yourself, Shad."

"Hustling—"

"Tea?" Emmett inquired nonchalantly from the other side of Morgan.

"That's right," Conrad responded. "She's drinking tea, Shad, not brandy. If you doubt me, take yourself a taste."

Morgan shook his head.

"That's a steep price to pay for tea," Emmett commented. "One whole dollar."

Maria spun around and was about to head for the table she had left earlier when Conrad reached out and seized her by the wrist. "Don't go, milady. Let's you and me talk business."

"Let me go!" she cried, struggling to free herself.

Conrad didn't. Instead, he pulled her close to him and his free hand eased into the bodice of her dress. She slapped his face, and he laughed. She swore at him in Spanish, and he laughed louder. But his laughter abruptly died when Morgan broke his grip on Maria's wrist and then landed a left on his jaw that sent him crashing down to the dirt floor, from which a small cloud of dust arose.

"Dammit, Shad, what the hell did you do that for?"

Conrad barked from where he lay on the floor. Rubbing his chin, he slowly got to his feet and stood facing Morgan.

"Leave her alone," Morgan ordered.

"What are you getting all riled up for, Shad?" Conrad asked in a placating tone. "She's just a—"

"That's enough, Ty!" Morgan warned. "Let's get out of here, miss." Before either Conrad or Emmett could say anything more, Morgan escorted Maria to the door.

"You may call me Maria, if you like," she told him as they emerged from the saloon. "May I call you Shad?"

"Sure you can. Listen, I'm awful sorry about the way my friend acted in there. I reckon it's on account of he's not been in the company of a lady in a real long time and he just forgot his manners there for a minute."

"You reminded him of them in quite a forceful way, I must say."

"I did?" Morgan broke into a smile. "Oh, I think I follow you. You're talking about how I hit him?"

Maria returned his smile as they walked away from the saloon. "I live up this way." She took his arm and led him through a tangle of tents. She stopped in front of one of them and turned to Morgan. "Thank you for coming to my rescue."

"You're welcome, I'm sure. This here's your place?"

"Yes."

Morgan hesitated, not sure what to do next, unable to make himself turn and walk away from Maria. "Do you mind if I ask you something personal?" When he saw the way her expression hardened following his question, he quickly added, "No, it's nothing like that. I mean—what I meant was—you speak real good English but you're Spanish, I take it."

Maria's expression slowly softened. "Yes, I am Spanish. That is to say I come from Old Mexico. And yes, I know how to speak good English. My father and mother, they worked at a large hacienda during my childhood. The owners were Mexicans but they also spoke English, and Doña Ana, the wife of Don Rodrigo, taught me to speak it, too, so that I would have an easier time of it in the world that was changing all around us. You see, Don Rodrigo and Doña Ana, they both knew that their day and their ways were coming to an end. Slowly to be sure, but ending nonetheless. They knew that the day of the gringo was about to dawn, and we Californios. . . ." She shrugged.

"Californios? You mean the Mexicans living here?"

"Yes. The Mexicans living here in what was once Mexican land."

Morgan heard the note of bitterness that had crept into Maria's voice, which had sounded, he thought, a little like the tolling of a badly cast bell.

"But now the kind señor wonders what a woman like me is doing here in a place like this. That is so, yes?"

"Well, the question did cross my mind, I have to admit."

"Gold. It is why I come—and stay—here." Maria stared defiantly at Morgan. "Oh, I do not pan for it. I do not crack gravel with a hammer in the hope of finding it. But I seek it. And I find it. In the pockets of men—so many men— like yourself. When I have much money—much gold—enough to buy for myself a better life— when that day comes, I will leave here. But until then, I do what I must—anything for the gold that, when it is mine, will let me leave here and leave behind me the Maria Almonte I was. Then, on that fine day, I will go to some other place where no one has ever heard of Maria Almonte, where no one will curl the lip and spit when they hear my name."

"You're not a whole lot different from me, Miss Almonte. I want to get rich and have myself a better life too. There's nothing wrong with that, so far as I can see."

Maria stared at Morgan for a silent minute before remarking, "You are a strange man, Mr. Shad Morgan. Or is it that you did not hear what I have just told you? Or perhaps you did not understand what it was that I was saying to you."

"The only thing I understand, Miss Almonte, is that meeting you was a pure pleasure for me, and I thank you for spending some time talking to me. I had me some worrisome times on my way here to California, but I have to tell you that meeting up with a woman like yourself, it made all those trying times well worthwhile. I hope you and me, we can get to be good friends."

"Friends? To be friends—that is all you want with Maria Almonte, Shad? Friendship?"

Morgan silently damned himself when he felt his face flush hotly. "I guess that's about it, Miss Almonte. I mean it is when you consider that though you sure are one fine figure of a woman —the kind that would make any man's heart hurry like you did mine the minute I laid eyes on you in the saloon back there—I know I'm not saying this right or putting my point plain— but the thing of it is, Miss Almonte—"

"Maria."

"The hard fact of the matter where you and me's concerned, Miss—I mean, Maria—is that I've not got any gold to give you. . . ."

Morgan fell silent as Maria, her face impassive, held out her hands to him. He looked down at them and then up at her. And then he took her hands in his and, as she stepped closer to him and kissed him on the lips, he closed his eyes. But he opened them when he felt her tugging at him and let her lead him into her tent, where, his heart hammering, he took her in his arms.

Hours later, Morgan returned to the saloon in search of Conrad and Emmett but found the establishment empty of customers. A question he put to the bartender elicited the information that Emmett had announced that he was leaving Grizzly Flats and that Conrad, like almost everyone else in the camp, had gone to trade with some men who had arrived in the area from Sacramento with a mule train. Morgan, following the bartender's directions, made his way to the site of the trading, where he found a jubilant Conrad, who proudly displayed what he had acquired from the mule train merchants.

"This tent—look at it, Shad. It's brand new,

with not a hole in it. It'll keep us dry and warm, and these provisions will keep our guts from growling like grizzlies."

"Ty, I'm sorry for hitting you the way I did. I guess my temper just got the best of me."

Conrad smiled and clapped Morgan on the shoulder. "I deserved it. I was out of line in the things I said. Only I didn't know you had an eye for the señorita."

"How much is my share of all this?" Morgan asked, and Conrad, after some quick calculations, told him.

Morgan paid his share, and then, as both men gathered up what Conrad had bought and went in search of a suitable place to pitch the tent that was to be their new home, Conrad commented, "Where've you been all this time, Shad? Or am I out of line for asking?"

"With Maria—Miss Almonte."

Conrad gave him a sage nod.

"She was telling me about how she's had a real hard life."

"It was easy to see that she took a fancy to you right from the start back there in the saloon. She never gave old Emmett or me so much as a glance. She only had eyes for you."

"Maybe she liked the way I was polite to her. It couldn't have been my looks that caught her eye, on account of nobody would be likely to call me the pick of the Morgan litter."

"Maybe that's true enough. But the fact remains you're not the kind of fellow that'd be hard on a lady's eyes. Not if she likes her fellas lean and hungry-looking and with the eyes of a lovesick calf."

Ten minutes later, Morgan halted. "What about right here, Ty? We're not far from water here, and over there's a good stand of timber we can cut for cooking fires. The land's level enough and it's not too rocky."

"Looks fine to me."

They set about pitching their tent, and when it was up, they entered it and told one another that it would make a fine home.

"It's far from the palaces we'll both build and live in when we strike it rich," Conrad remarked in an amused tone, "but it's snug enough."

The dawn found them trudging eagerly along the bank of the American River as they searched for a spot to begin the day's digging. They found one a little while later that was deserted and shaded by a stand of willows growing on the bank, with their branches drifting gracefully down toward the water.

They spent the day, except for a brief break

for a meal when the sun reached its meridian, panning in the cold river. By the time the sun was setting, they had, to their mutual delight, gathered gold that they estimated would be worth close to forty dollars.

On their way back to the camp, Morgan proposed an idea. "We ought to build ourselves a sluice like the ones I saw some of the other fellows using," he suggested. "We could, had we one of them, go through a whole lot more dirt in a whole lot less time. Which, the way I figure it, ought to increase our chances of finding gold —and even increase the odds on how much we can find between the two of us. What do you say, Ty?"

"I say sure, though we'll have to lay out some more cash money for the tools and things we'll need to build a sluice. But I guess it's a worthy investment."

"My purse is almost as flat as an apple stepped on by an elephant, but I do think building ourselves a sluice is worth the gamble when you stack it up against the cash outlay it'll take us to make one."

They spent the next several days acquiring what they needed to build their sluice and then putting the device together. When Morgan had hammered the last nail into the wooden apparatus, he stood up, and he and Conrad beamed at one another.

The sluice they had jointly constructed was a flat wooden trough, built on a slant, with a shallow hopper on the higher end and wooden strips, or riffles, nailed across the floor.

They carried it upriver then, past the spot where they had been prospecting the day before, and immediately set to work. Taking turns with a wheelbarrow they had bought, they hauled dirt they dug from the river bottom to the sluice and poured it into the hopper. The hopper's wire mesh, the riddle, screened out stones and pebbles. They doused the dirt with buckets of water, washing sand out of the sluice. Left behind was the heavier, possibly gold-bearing sediment, which was caught behind the riffles. They took turns sifting the sediment, and by the end of their first day's labor they had gathered what a discouraged Conrad estimated was less than twenty dollars' worth of gold.

"Luck's just not with us, Shad," he complained. "We spend the day, most of it, working like slaves and what have we got to show for it? Eighteen, nineteen dollars, that's all."

"We'll just have to keep at it," Morgan said. "Our luck's bound to change." But secretly he doubted his own words. Because, he thought, a man's luck can run bad for a long time before it changes—if it ever does. There was just no way of getting around that hard fact. Hard work wasn't enough. Not in the diggings. A man could work his butt off and break his back and he might not find a speck of color ever, while another man might literally stumble over gold-bearing rock. He recalled Ty's find, which had resulted from the man having kicked a rock to reveal the presence of a gold nugget hidden beneath it.

"Let's call it a day, Shad," Conrad wearily suggested.

They did, and that night Conrad visited the saloon, returning roaring drunk an hour before dawn to the tent he shared with Morgan.

The next morning Morgan went back to the spot he had worked with Conrad the day before, to find several other men panning the river not far away. He went up to them. "You boys having any luck?"

Heads shook as the men continued working.

Morgan pulled his leather pouch from his pocket. "Me and my partner came up with close to twenty dollars' worth of gold yesterday, which we took out of the river downstream aways."

"You're telling the truth?" one man asked skeptically. "You're not joshing us?"

"It's the truth I'm telling you."

"Did you record your claim?" one of the men asked him.

"Record it?"

"Sure, you got to record your claim else somebody's liable to jump it. If you've found gold, well, fella, you better hurry up and record your claim."

"How do I go about doing that?"

"The claim recorder's the saloonkeeper in Grizzly Flats. Our rules in the flats regarding placer mining claims is a man's got the right to claim twenty feet along the bank of a waterway and out as far as the middle of a wide river like the American. On cricks, a claim can run all the way from one bank to the other. You've got to mark your claim with your name and stake out its boundaries. Then, like I said, you got to make sure it's recorded."

"I'm obliged to you for the information."

"Are you sure you're not joshing us about finding gold? We've not found so much as a flake."

Morgan opened his pouch and emptied its gritty contents into his palm, which he proudly held out for the other men to see.

They gathered around him, and then one of the men snorted derisively. "That there's what you're bragging about?"

"Well, I'm willing to admit this little bit's not worth a whole lot, but it's better than nothing a'tall."

"Sonny, that what you're holding—it *is* nothing a'tall."

"What are you talking about?"

"That there's not gold. What it is is fool's gold."

"What do you mean, fool's gold?"

"Iron pyrites is what you've found, with some mica mixed in it."

Morgan looked down at the nuggets in his palm.

"Oh, it looks a lot like gold, I'll grant you. Greenhorns usually can't tell the difference till they've been in the diggings awhile. But gold don't glitter like pyrites does. It won't break if it's pounded, and that stuff will. Try it and see."

Morgan hesitated and then used his hammer to pound one of the nuggets on the top of a flat stone. It shattered into dust. He looked up at the men, who were laughing at him.

One of them fell silent and then said, "Don't let your mistake discourage you, son. You just keep at it. We all of us live and learn. Sometimes the school of life learns us a hard lesson."

Morgan watched the men walk away, some of them still laughing, and then he returned to his sluice. He was hard at work when, in the middle of the afternoon, Conrad appeared.

"My head feels like a horse stepped on it," he moaned and began to fill the wheelbarrow with dirt he shoveled up from the river bottom.

"Ty, I got some bad news to give you."

Conrad looked at him uneasily.

"What we found yesterday—it's not real gold. It's called fool's gold. It's iron pyrites with some mica mixed in."

"How do you know?"

"I talked to some fellows this morning who were working nearby. They told me. They said real gold couldn't be broken but fool's gold could be. I hammered one of our nuggets. It turned into dust."

"Maybe those fellows you met were lying to you so you'd leave here and they could lay claim to our spot."

"They weren't."

"You can't prove they weren't."

"I reckon I can. That nugget you found. Where is it?"

When Conrad produced the nugget from his

pocket, Morgan wordlessly handed him their hammer.

Conrad got down on one knee and then, after a brief moment's hesitation, brought the hammer down on the nugget he had placed on a stone. It flattened under the hammer but didn't break.

"Damn it to hell!" Conrad muttered, rising and pocketing his nugget.

Morgan went back to work.

Conrad didn't. He announced that in his opinion, they were wasting their time and making damned fools of themselves into the bargain. "I'm going back to Grizzly Flats," he declared. "I need a drink."

Morgan tried dissuading him, but Conrad was adamant. When he had gone, cursing under his breath, Morgan moved the sluice a half-mile upriver and continued working. By the end of the day, he had found in the sediment he had scraped from behind the sluice's riffles and then panned several small nuggets, none of them bigger than a trouser button. But he had bitten down on them and knew that they were gold. His delight was so great that he was able to forget his aching arms, his skinned knuckles, and the stiff muscles in the back of his legs and his lower back. He wanted to tell someone, wanted to whoop with joy. He did neither. Silently he staked out a twenty-foot stretch along the riverbank and left his tools as further proof that he was working that part of the river before returning to Grizzly Flats, where he found a drunken Conrad in the saloon.

"This is for real, Ty," he eagerly told his partner as he emptied his pouch on the bar. "It's the real true stuff." He picked up a nugget and bit down hard upon it, after which he proudly displayed the bent but unbroken lump to Conrad.

"Congratulations, Shad. That nugget, it's worth maybe ten dollars. And how long, my good friend, did it take you to earn that much money? All day it took you, didn't it?"

Morgan nodded.

"You might as well play a game of faro as pan for gold. You'll have as much chance of getting rich at one as the other. Come on. I'll prove my point to you."

Morgan tried to dissuade him, but Conrad ignored him and made his way to a nearby table, where a brisk game of faro was in progress. He watched as Conrad exchanged his gold nugget for a pile of chips, and he continued watching as Conrad placed five of his chips on the reproduction of the trey printed on the board.

The dealer dealt the first of a pair of cards from his dealing box. A ten. He dealt the second. The trey.

Conrad let out a victorious roar and collected the chips the dealer placed on his winning card. He glanced up at the casekeeper, the device that kept track of dealt cards, and immediately placed ten chips on the queen, which the casekeeper indicated had not yet appeared in the game.

The dealer dealt. Eight. Queen.

This time Conrad's roar almost brought the ridgepole crashing down on the players. He gathered his winnings and glanced again at the casekeeper. "Lookee, Shad, the nine's not shown up yet. What do you say? You want to put some money on the nine?"

Morgan was keenly conscious of his dwindling stake, and although he was sorely tempted to try to match the ease with which Conrad was winning, he reluctantly shook his head.

Conrad put his money on the nine. Then, apparently changing his mind, he switched to the king.

The king was the first card dealt.

Conrad continued playing, pausing only long enough to make an occasional quick trip to the bar for a drink. His lucky streak continued, and he again urged Morgan to play, but Morgan again refused. Later, when Conrad lost four times in succession, Morgan suggested that his luck had run out and that it was time to quit. Conrad would have none of it. He bet on the queen again and lost. On the next deal, he increased the number of chips he wagered—this time on the deuce—and lost again. Ten minutes later, his last chip found its way into the faro dealer's hands.

Conrad stood staring down at the faro board, his lips twisting, his eyes blinking.

"Let's go, Ty."

Conrad let Morgan lead him from the faro table. But halfway to the door he halted. "I need a drink."

"You don't, Ty. You need some rest so you'll be fit for work in the morning."

"What are you talking about, work in the morning, damn you? I'm not busting my back working that sluice anymore. I'm through. You saw how I was doing at the faro table. I was doing good—real good, dammit. I will again. I've still got a few dollars left. I—"

"*Step on up here, gentlemen, and try your luck!*"

Conrad turned at the sound of the loud and

oddly seductive male voice that had made itself heard above the din of the saloon.

"No marked cards in this game, gentlemen," the voice continued from the midst of a crowd gathered at the far end of the saloon. "No short decks, no humbug, just a straightforward chance for any man with a sharp pair of eyes to win himself a fortune at my expense."

"Come on, Shad."

Conrad went hurrying away from Morgan, who hesitated a moment and then followed Conrad as he made his way into the crowd. When Morgan had shouldered his way through the men gathered around the smooth-tongued talker, he stopped and stared in astonishment.

"Step right up, gentlemen! You see here the simple tools of my trade. Three products of the walnut tree. And here I have a piece of cork no bigger than a pea. Now the task before you gentlemen is simplicity itself. Watch me closely. I place this cork under this walnut shell and then —are you watching closely, gentlemen?—I shift the three walnut shells about like this and then it is all up to you. Place your wagers on which shell you believe harbors the cork. If you select the right one on the first try, you win."

"I've never yet beat one of these thimbleriggers," muttered a man next to Morgan. "They're way too slick for me."

Conrad put a dollar down on the thimblerigger's table and pointed to the walnut shell on the left.

With a flourish, the thimblerigger lifted the shell to reveal the presence of the piece of cork beneath it. "My congratulations, sir," he said to Conrad. "You have a sharp eye which may very well bankrupt me."

Conrad beamed at the thimblerigger. He took the dollar the man handed him.

Morgan's gaze was on the clean-shaven lantern-jawed man, anger surging inside him. He tried but failed to catch the man's glittering eyes, one of which was blue, the other gray.

"Now, gentlemen, you have all seen how easy it is to beat me at my own game. But I must warn you. I have not surrendered yet. I intend to try to recoup my losses and then some, to be quite frank with you. To that end, I am now prepared to bet six dollars to one dollar on the next round."

The thimblerigger's offer was greeted with applause and the placing of a flurry of bets. But no one won because, when the thimblerigger lifted the walnut shell the men had bet on, there was no piece of cork beneath it.

Groans. But then, quickly, more bets, followed as quickly by more losses.

Morgan, watching the thimblerigger's fingers dance lightly about on his board as he twisted and shifted his three walnut shells, suddenly caught his breath. When he was certain of what he was seeing, he reached out and seized the thimblerigger's wrist. "Hold it!"

The eager gamblers surrounding Morgan let out a series of indignant protests concerning the interruption of the game. The thimblerigger swore and tried to free himself from Morgan's grip but failed to do so.

"You boys are being played for fools," Morgan told the angry gamblers.

"Let him be!" ordered a scowling man who was standing beside Morgan.

"Don't be a spoilsport," another snapped.

"This here game's as crooked as the last letter of the alphabet," Morgan told the men.

"What are you talking about, Shad?" Conrad asked.

"Pick up those shells, Ty," Morgan ordered, still gripping the thimblerigger's wrist.

Conrad, a puzzled frown on his face, did so.

An angry murmur ran through the crowd when the gamblers saw that there was no piece of cork under any of the three walnut shells.

"Where the hell is it?" Conrad bellowed, voicing the question that was on the minds of the other gamblers.

Morgan slammed the thimblerigger's hand down on the board, and as he did so, the missing piece of cork popped out from between two of the man's fingers, rolled across the board, and fell to the floor.

"How did you know—" Conrad began.

"By keeping a sharp eye on this fellow," Morgan replied. "It took me awhile but I finally saw what he was up to. When one of you boys'd point to a shell in the belief that it was the one the cork was under, this here fellow, as he lifted the shell, made his fast move. He caught up the cork between his two fingers before anyone watching was any the wiser. So the man who picked the right shell wound up a loser anyway."

"But I won the first time I played," Conrad pointed out, and then, seeing the amused expression on Morgan's face, he clapped a hand to his forehead and cried, "I get it. He *let* me win to keep me at the game."

"You got it, Ty," Morgan said.

"We ought to string him up," one of the men muttered.

"Get a rope!" somebody at the rear of the crowd yelled.

The thimblerigger's eyes went wide with fear. He struck out with his suddenly fisted free hand and delivered a sharp blow to Morgan's jaw. Then, jerking himself free of Morgan, he made a run for the door. But Morgan quickly recovered from the blow and went after him. He caught up with him at the door of the saloon, spun him around, and pinned both of his arms behind his back. "Back off!" he yelled to the advancing tide of angry gamblers. "This man's mine!"

"Like hell he is!" one of the men yelled. "You didn't lose even a dime to him."

"You're wrong on that score, mister," Morgan said. "I lost twenty-five hard-earned dollars to this man, only it wasn't here that I lost it. I mean to get it back."

The gamblers halted, muttering uncertainly among themselves.

"What's your name, mister?" Morgan asked his prisoner.

"None of your damned business!"

"His name's Jack Borden," one of the gamblers volunteered. "He was running the same shell game over at Ophir a while back."

Morgan released Borden, who turned to face him. "The last time we met it was on board the *Eagle*. You were calling yourself Dr. White then and you charged me twenty-five dollars for passage up the Chagres River to Panama City. Only that was the last I ever saw you—and the money I paid you."

"You've got me mixed up with somebody else," Borden protested.

"No, I don't. Oh, you were wearing a beard when you called yourself Dr. White. But I remember your eyes being two different colors—one blue and one gray. Now I want my money back, Borden, and I reckon these boys you cheated in your shell game, they no doubt want their money back too."

Borden lunged for the door.

Morgan seized him by the shoulder before he had taken two steps and slammed him up against the wall. Drawing his Colt from his waistband, Morgan said, "Hand over my money or I'll start shooting off your ears."

"Don't! I'll give you the money. Only don't shoot!"

Minutes later, Morgan had his twenty-five dollars back and the gamblers had also had the money they had lost at Borden's shell game returned to them.

"Where's that rope?" one of the men in the crowd suddenly shouted.

Morgan quickly shoved Borden out the door.

As Borden fled into the night, Morgan, blocking the door with his body and holding his gun almost nonchalantly in his right hand, said, "You boys don't want to wind up the night as the murderers of a tinhorn gambler, now do you? After all, you've got your money back, and the night's young and the bar's still well stocked."

"You're aiding and abetting that bastard's escape!" screeched an irate gambler.

"If any of you boys should ever run into Jack Borden again, you can alert everybody to the fact that he's a crook. That ought to keep him from cheating anybody else. And that, I reckon, ought to be enough to satisfy the lot of you." Morgan's gun barrel rose. His finger tightened on the gun's trigger.

The crowd surged toward him and then abruptly halted. A man muttered something unintelligible before turning and heading back to the bar. Slowly the crowd began to dissolve. Minutes later, as Morgan thrust his .31 back into his waistband, it was business as usual in the saloon.

# SIX

On his way out of Grizzly Flats the next morning, Morgan met Maria Almonte in front of a shack that bore a sign identifying it as a restaurant.

"You are a hero now, yes, Shad?" Maria said after they had exchanged greetings.

"Hero? Me? You must have me mixed up with somebody else, Maria."

"I hear about what happened last night in the saloon. How you chase away the bad man named Borden."

"Oh, that." Morgan grinned. "That weren't but a case of clearing out a pesky polecat and as little worthy of mention."

"That is not what the men say who saw what happened."

"It's not?"

"They say you showed no fear in the face of this Borden who had two guns to your one. They say you stood up to him when he tried to slash you with his long knife. They say you are a very brave man."

"Maria, you oughtn't to pay attention to such fanciful tales. Now I'll tell you the truth. Jack Borden wasn't armed. He had no guns to go up against mine. What's more, he had no knife."

"So the men were wrong when they talked of Borden's weapons. Were they wrong, I wonder, when they said you were brave?"

"A man does what he has to do, and sometimes that makes him seem brave when all he really is, some folks would say, is bullheaded enough not to let anybody stomp on him."

Maria smiled. She put a hand on Morgan's cheek and gently stroked it. "I have missed you."

Morgan covered her hand with his own.

And then, before he could say anything, she withdrew her hand and was gone.

He continued on his way in the midst of a crowd of other prospectors on their way to the diggings. One of them asked him how his luck was holding.

"Barely," he answered with a smile.

"Me and two of my friends have a two-hundred-foot sluice up the line aways. What brought us to Grizzly Flats from over by Rich Bar was the wild tales men everywhere were telling about men hitting it big here. But when we got here, we heard it was just a single strike some lucky so-and-so made somewhere up in the hills."

"I heard about that one too," Morgan said. "A man they say went up into the hills between here and the Sierra Nevada and came down with nearly seven hundred dollars' worth of ore. Everybody said he was crazy when he went into the hills, but they thought he was smart as a whip when he came down out of them."

"Which just goes to prove that gold is where you find it."

"They say that fellow, when he went back into the hills after a week-long bender, never could find the spot again where he'd made his strike."

"Poor devil."

"Little drops of water,
Little grains of gold,
Make our bellies full of
All the grub they'll hold."

Morgan walked on, smiling at the variation on the old childhood song that he had heard for the first time following Borden's departure from the saloon the night before, which now was being sung by one of the men in the crowd.

"Little pails of water,
     Little pans of sand . . ."

Morgan added his voice to the jaunty voices of the other men:

"Make the damnedest blisters
     Come on every hand."

"Lord a'mercy, ain't that the sad truth though," groaned his companion. "Since I come out here from Kansas, I been cracking quartz and panning riverbeds and burrowing my way down to bedrock from here to Hades and back again, and so far I've raised seventy-five dollars' worth of gold and blisters on both hands, both feet, and both knees." The man laughed unroariously. "But I've not got a single blister on my butt, which is dumb testimony to my dogged determination to get rich."

Morgan found himself thinking of Ty Conrad and wondering what had become of Conrad's determination to become rich. He seemed to have abandoned the idea. He seemed content now to spend his time drinking and gambling in the saloon. This morning when Morgan awoke, he had found that he was alone in the tent, which made him wonder if Conrad was still in the saloon, which never seemed to close.

"A friend of mine," continued Morgan's companion as the two men trudged along, "gave up any hope of finding gold. He hitched up his oxen and headed back home to Kansas. Sometimes I think he might have done the smart thing. Sometimes I think there's something a little silly about grown men mucking about in the dirt like we do, looking for pieces of some shiny metal that'll make our fondest dreams come true."

"Something like this don't happen but once in a man's lifetime," Morgan remarked. "When I first heard about it, I started chomping at the bit to set out for California."

"You don't ever get discouraged?"

"I do. But I was never much of a scholar. I reckon maybe I'm just too slow-witted to learn the lesson that not all of us out here—in fact only a few of us—are going to get rich."

"Well, here's where I part company with you. Me and my friends are digging up around the bend yonder."

"Good luck to you," Morgan said, and the man waved, wished him luck in return, and moved away.

When Morgan reached his claim, which was identified as his because of the presence of his sluice, wheelbarrow, and tools on it, he went right to work. He soon found that without Conrad's help, the job of shoveling the dirt into the sluice, pouring on the water, and then rocking the sluice was doubly hard. But he did it, the task quickly becoming a monotonous routine. Shovel. Pour. Rock. Shovel, pour, rock. Shovel . . .

Morgan looked up when he heard the sound of someone angrily shouting in the distance. Moments later he saw three men, one of whom was the man who had accompanied him to the diggings earlier, round a distant bend and come running down a low slope toward the spot where a number of other prospectors were working their claims. He watched as the three men stopped to talk to the prospectors. As he continued watching, he saw the prospectors bend and begin to examine their riffle boxes before turning and heading in his direction.

When the small crowd of men reached Morgan, the one Morgan knew, without preamble, bellowed, "Somebody's been stealing gold out of our sluice boxes. You lost any?"

"No," Morgan answered. "How do you know that thieving's going on around here?"

"We left some nuggets in our riffle boxes overnight. This morning those nuggets were gone. Somebody made off with them during the night."

"These three fellows told us what had happened," one of the other men said. "We checked our sluices and sure enough some of our gold was gone too. We've got to do something to stop the thieving, that's for sure."

"Post a guard to stand watch at night when there's nobody about," Morgan advised. "Set up a fund to pay for the man's services."

"That's not a bad idea," said the man who had earlier accompanied Morgan to the diggings. "By the way, my name's Chilton. What's yours?"

"Shad Morgan."

"Morgan," repeated one of the other men in the crowd. "That's him, boys. I thought he looked familiar. He's the one who ran Jack Borden out of Grizzly Flats when he caught that thimblerigger cheating in the saloon last night."

"Morgan's idea," Chilton said, "sounds like a good one to me. What do you say, boys? Shall we hire ourselves a guard?"

Morgan stood watching as the men turned away, fanned out, and began talking to other prospectors in the area. Then, seeking a change of pace, he spent the next hour cleaning his sluice.

He removed the sediment lodged behind each of the riffles in his sluice, sifting it carefully, hoping to catch a glint of gold. When he was finished cleaning the riffle box, he had gathered, with painstaking effort, only a few flakes of gold, which were worth, he estimated, somewhere in the neighborhood of twenty dollars.

Suppressing his strong feelings of discouragement that bordered on depression, he shoveled more dirt from the bottom of the river into his wheelbarrow and trundled it up to the sluice. After dumping it into the hopper, he filled two buckets with water and poured them over the dirt. Using a stick, he stirred the mixture and watched the water flow out of the lower end of the riffle box, leaving behind it sediment trapped by the riffles.

"Hey, you, Morgan!"

He straightened and saw several men, Chilton leading them, coming toward him. When they reached him, Chilton announced, "We've talked to every prospector for a mile in every direction and every man jack of them wants to hire a guard, because most of them, it turns out, have lost gold during the night same as we did. But none of the men we talked to wants to be that guard. They're all too hell-bent on digging. But they did pay their share of a bounty we decided to raise to pay the guard we hire—if he catches the thief that's on the prowl amongst us. We've got close to a thousand dollars. What about you? Do you want the job of guarding our gold?"

Morgan, surprised by the offer, hesitated. He looked down at the sediment in his sluice box. He could see no sign of color in it. A thousand dollars, he thought. A sure thing, he thought. The thousand-dollar bounty, he thought, it's not a gamble like digging in the dirt for gold is. That much money would grubstake me for a good long time if I'm frugal. But then there's another side to the story, he reminded himself, still staring down at his unprofitable sluice box. Granted that hunting gold's a gamble, a man could make a whole lot more than a thousand dollars if he has a little bit of luck and if time's on his side.

"I do thank you gents for offering me the job," he told the waiting men. "But I think I'll stick to prospecting."

The men, obviously disappointed, spent several minutes trying to persuade him to change his mind. When they failed to do so, they stated their intention to send a delegate to town with the authority to hire a guard to protect their sluice boxes.

"I want to pay my share toward the bounty," Morgan told them. "How much is it?"

"Twenty dollars," Chilton told him. "And it'll be worth every penny. *If* we can find ourselves a guard. And *if* he can catch our thief."

Morgan paid his twenty dollars and, as the men left, returned to work.

He was still working when the sun went down, without having found any gold. As the shadows thickened around him, making it hard to see, he gave it up for the day and started back to Grizzly Flats.

When he reached the shantytown, it was dark. He made his way to his tent, where he was surprised to find Conrad hunkered down outside it in front of a fire.

"Figured you'd be along about now," Conrad greeted him. "Light and take a load off your feet. I've got beans in the pot and salt pork in the frying pan. You hungry?"

"I sure am. My belly's growling louder than a grizzly." Morgan gave Conrad a sidelong glance. "I missed you up at the diggings today."

"I've been meaning to talk to you about that, Shad. I've had me a belly full of grubbing about in the dirt. I think it's high time you found yourself another partner—if you want one."

"What do you have in mind to do instead of prospecting, Ty?"

Conrad took a tin plate and spooned beans and salt pork into it. "I got me a job," he declared proudly as he handed the plate to Morgan.

"A job? What kind of a job?"

"You're looking at a just-hatched bounty hunter, Shad."

Morgan chewed, swallowed, and, pointing his spoon at Conrad, said, "You took the guard job that bunch of miners were offering, did you?"

"You just bet your boots I did. For a thousand dollars—maybe more if more prospectors pitch in their share of the cost of protecting their sluice boxes—I'd be a fool not to take it." Conrad forked food into his mouth and then did the almost impossible: he grinned and chewed at the same time. "I was over in the saloon when those fellows showed up looking for a man to hire."

"What are they counting on doing to the thief if they—if you catch him?"

"We'll hang him."

Morgan lowered his eyes and continued eating in silence.

"There's no telling where this thing might lead, Shad." Conrad speculated. "I mean if I do catch the gold thief, well, folks are bound to hear about it, and with all the rowdies and roughnecks that are pouring into Grizzly Flats, maybe they'll want to pay me to protect their businesses from any possible harm at the hands of the ne'er-do-wells."

"Maybe they will, Ty."

"A job like that—and like the one I've got at the moment—they're more my style. You know, brain work rather than backbreaking work like prospecting."

"I wish you luck, Ty. If I'd of known you'd be interested in the job of guard, I'd have mentioned you to those fellows when they offered me the job of looking after their sluice boxes at night."

"They offered you the job too? They did say they'd offered it to a whole pot full of fellows before they got around to me."

Morgan nodded.

"I can't understand why you—why all the others too—didn't jump at the chance to earn that thousand-dollar bounty."

Morgan shrugged. Smiled. "Me and all those other fellows, I reckon we've all caught ourselves bad cases of gold fever. You—well, it does seem as if you escaped the epidemic."

Both men continued eating in silence. They

were almost finished with their meal when a figure materialized out of the darkness and strode toward them.

Morgan looked up and then down at his food. He looked up again, squinting in the firelight. And then, dropping his plate and spoon, he leapt to his feet and threw his arms around the man who had emerged from the darkness, exclaiming, "Cass Jamieson! Hey, it's good to see you! Where did you come from? When did you get here? What—"

Laughing, Jamieson held up a hand to silence the excited Morgan. "One question at a time, Shad. Let's sit down here and I'll do my best to fill you in on what's been happening to me since we parted in Panama City." Jamieson hunkered down by the fire. "Good to see you again, Ty."

"Same here, Jamieson. You're all over the fever, are you?"

"I am."

"When did you get to California?" Morgan asked Jamieson.

"Day before yesterday," was the answer. "I set out right away for the American River. You told me, Shad, that that's where you might be found. On my way, I had the good fortune to run into some fellows who were talking about you, which is how I found out where you were."

"About me?"

"About how you bested that fellow—what was his name?—the man who was running that crooked shell game here in Grizzly Flats."

"Jack Borden."

"The men I met—Shad, they were singing your praises to high heaven. One of them said, as I recall, that if Grizzly Flats ever grew big enough to need a mayor, you ought to be it."

"Maybe I could make out better being a mayor than being a miner."

Conrad got to his feet. "I've got to be going. I'll see you boys later."

"Where are you going, Ty?" Jamieson asked.

"I've got me a job night guarding some miners' sluice boxes," Conrad answered. "Some of the boys have lost gold out of their boxes, so they've hired me to put a stop to the thieving. They're all set to pay me a thousand dollars if I can do that. It's a job that beats busting your knuckles and kneecaps digging for gold."

"It also sounds like it might be a dangerous job," Jamieson ventured.

Conrad displayed a gun in a shoulder holster that had been hidden inside his coat. "I bought me this to make it less dangerous."

When Conrad had gone, Morgan said, "Ty and me, we were partners for a time. But it seems he's given up the notion of trying to dig gold out of the ground."

"I take it, Shad, that you've not had the best of luck in your prospecting, judging by your earlier remark about possibly making out better as a mayor than as a miner."

"You take it right. But I keep at it. One of these days. . . ."

"You sound like almost every man I've met on my way here. They're all counting on striking it rich someday. Not many of them do, from what I've heard. In fact, most of them never do find their personal El Dorado. They wind up heading back to the States with nothing more to show for their efforts than worn-out shoes falling off their feet and a hangdog look on their faces."

"The same thing might happen to me in the end," Morgan reluctantly admitted. "But I'm not ready to throw in the towel—not yet, I'm not. What about you, Cass? What are you going to do now that you're here? If you mean to dig for gold—I could use a partner."

"I'm not sure just what I'm going to do, Shad. I think I'll just have a look around for a while and see how the land lies before I make a move. It seems to me that a man with some gumption and a dash of imagination ought to be able to find himself some kind of paying proposition out here in the diggings."

"Something akin to selling steamship tickets at a hefty profit, you mean?"

Jamieson frowned. "You think there was something wrong with what I did back in Panama? Well, I can tell you there wasn't. I broke no laws. I didn't cheat anybody, like that Borden fellow you routed out of here did. I—"

Morgan held up a hand. "Whoa, Cass! I'm not finding fault with what you did. I just happened to mention it, is all. I didn't mean no offense."

Jamieson's expression gradually softened. "No offense taken. Say, what are we sitting here jabbering like this for? Let's go someplace convivial. I have the local saloon in mind, of course. There's whiskey there and at least one woman— a señorita named Maria."

"You met up with Maria?"

"I went to the saloon to ask where I might find you, and she gave me directions to your tent. So what do you say, Shad? Will you let me buy you a drink to celebrate our reunion?"

Morgan nodded. "Sure I will. If you'll let me buy you one."

After Morgan had kicked out the campfire, they headed for the saloon.

"I don't mean to press the issue, Shad, or pry. But I'm as curious as the proverbial cat. Have you found any gold at all?"

"Ty and I found some. A little less than a hundred dollars' worth apiece, all told."

"That's not much, if you don't mind my saying so."

"I know it's not."

"Then why do you keep at it?"

"I don't rightly know how to answer that question, Cass. I guess there are a lot of answers to it, come to think about it. Like what else is a fellow like me—a clodhopper with high hopes but no education worth speaking about—to do but try to better himself out here in the diggings. Then there's the fact that I am, after all, here. I guess when you come right down to it, what I'm saying is I don't want to give up, not without a fight.

"And the fight out here is just to keep on panning, digging, and hoping. Every day when I go out to the river, I tell myself this is the day. This will be the day I'll strike paydirt. It's a funny thing about prospecting for gold, Cass. It's a way of life that worms its way into a man's blood and brain. It drives him hard. It keeps him going, keeps him at it. What it really is, it's a dream, Cass. A dream that keeps calling to a man and keeps him chasing it day after day while he tries his damnedest to make it come true for him."

"There she is," Jamieson breathed as they entered the saloon a few minutes later. "She's some package, isn't she, Shad?"

Morgan stared through the smoke at Maria Almonte, who, with castanets in both hands, was dancing on top of a table while men hooted and caterwauled their noisy approval of her performance.

Morgan followed Jamieson to the bar, where both men ordered whiskey. When they had been served, they turned to watch Maria.

Her skirts whirled stormily around her lithe legs. Her hair, unbound, swirled about her head as she twisted, writhed, wriggled, and turned, the castanets her only accompaniment. And then suddenly it was over. The castanets fell silent. Maria, her chest heaving and her dark eyes glowing in the flickering light of the coal oil lamps, bowed her acknowledgment of the crowd's applause and shouted approval before stepping down onto a chair and then down upon the saloon's straw-strewn dirt floor.

She eluded one man's eager grasp and, laughing, made her way through the crowd toward the bar. She halted when she noticed Morgan.

Their eyes met, and then she moved through the smoky air and took up a position between Morgan and Jamieson.

"I see your friend has found you," she said to Morgan with a casual glance in Jamieson's direction.

"He did. How are you, Maria?"

"Well. And you, Shad—how goes it with you?"

"Not bad. The fellows in here, they sure do like the way you dance."

Maria tossed her long black hair in a dismissive gesture that was almost contemptuous. "I do not care about them. What did you think? Did *you* like the way I danced?"

"*I* certainly did," Jamieson stated enthusiastically before Morgan could respond to the question. "In fact, I'm quite certain I'd like just about anything you did, Maria. You don't mind if I call you Maria, do you, honey?"

She did not answer the question. Instead, she put a hand on Morgan's forearm and whispered, "Do you want to come with me?"

Morgan turned and set his glass down on the bar. He took Maria's hand and was about to make his way through the crowd with her when Jamieson stepped in front of him.

"You two aren't leaving so soon, are you? I

mean, the night's young and rich with promise."

"Excuse me, señor," Maria said, trying to
step around Jamieson. "I must go."

"Let the lady through, Cass," Morgan said in
a low tone.

"Sure I will, Shad." Jamieson stepped back.
"The way's clear, honey. But before you go—"

Maria remained motionless, waiting for Jamieson to go on.

"—give a listen to what I've got to say to
you," Jamieson concluded, his eager eyes
bluntly appraising her shapely body.

Morgan, annoyance building within him,
said, "Speak your piece, Cass, and be done with
it. The lady and I are leaving."

Jamieson's glance flicked from Maria to Morgan and back again. "How much is he paying
you?" he asked her.

Morgan reached out and shoved Jamieson out
of his way. "Come on, Maria."

But before either of them could take a single
step, Jamieson, addressing Maria, said, "I'll pay
you double whatever he's paying you."

A cold glint hardened Maria's eyes. "You are
a fool, señor. He pays me nothing."

Jamieson's eyebrows arched in disbelief. "Is

that a fact? Well, it does seem that you've captured the lady's fancy, Shad."

As Morgan stepped around him and began to lead Maria toward the door, Jamieson turned and called out, "Twenty dollars."

Morgan was brought to an abrupt halt when Maria suddenly stopped.

Then she moved quickly ahead of Morgan, hurrying toward the door, her hand still in his.

"Fifty!" Jamieson called out to her.

She slowed and let go of Morgan's hand. She turned.

So did Morgan.

Both of them stared in silence at the leering Jamieson, who stood with his back to the bar, his elbows resting on it. He raised one arm and crooked a finger, beckoning to Maria.

She hesitated a moment and then, giving Morgan the briefest of shamefaced glances, made her way toward Jamieson.

"You see, Shad?" he called out merrily. "Friendship's a fine thing. So is love. But what it all comes down to in the ugly end is the almighty dollar. Isn't that true, my high-priced little lady?"

Maria remained silent as she stood facing Jamieson, her arms at her sides and her shoulders slumped in an attitude of complete defeat.

Morgan strode across the room that was now silent as all the men in it intently watched the proceedings. "Maria, I want you to go with me. I want—"

Jamieson interrupted him. "What you want is of no importance, Shad. What is important—and it's high time you learned this bitter lesson—is not what a man wants but how much he can *pay* for what he wants. Now I'm willing to pay top dollar for Maria. I'm willing to wager that she will take me up on my offer. An offer, I should add, you are perfectly willing, though possibly not able, to match. Am I right, Maria?"

Maria drew a deep breath. She avoided looking at Morgan. "You are right, señor," she told Jamieson in a small voice.

Someone in the crowd snickered.

Morgan turned and left the saloon.

In the days that followed, Morgan stayed away from the saloon, knowing that he was really staying away not from the saloon but from Maria. The image of Jamieson's mocking expression as he offered Maria more money than she had the strength to refuse was burned into his memory. When he first heard the rumors involving Maria, he didn't believe them—didn't want to believe them. But he soon came to know they were true. Jamieson was now living with Maria and taking a sixty percent share of her earnings.

Morgan continued working the American River, but he never found more than four dollars' worth of gold per day, and often his take was considerably less. What he did find he had to sell to pay his expenses. There was no money to send home to Connecticut.

Conrad continued guarding the sluice boxes of the miners who had hired him, but, as he complained more than once to Morgan, "No matter how diligent I am, whoever it is that's stealing the gold still manages to get past me." Gold, according to Conrad, continued to disappear from the sluices even though many of the miners had begun the unusual practice of cleaning their boxes each night instead of only on Saturdays, as had previously been the custom.

"At this rate," he declared one sunny morning as Morgan was getting ready to leave the tent they shared, "I'll never see that thousand dollar-bounty I was offered for catching the thief."

Morgan expressed sympathy for Ty's plight, but secretly he couldn't help wondering if sympathy was really called for in the situation, since Conrad continued to spend freely in the saloon, the restaurant, and several of the gambling tents that had sprung up in Grizzly Flats.

As he ducked under the tent flap and stepped outside into the crisp breeze sweeping down from the snow-clad peaks of the Sierra Nevada mountains, Ty followed him.

"What I need is some of the slick skills of a man like our friend Jamieson. Have you heard about his latest scheme?"

Morgan shook his head.

"Jamieson's been buying out claims—rich ones. Then he hires men to work them for him for a percentage of the profits. A percentage that is, I hear, a low one. Some say he pays only thirty percent. But there's a bunch of fellows here in the flats who'd rather take thirty percent of something than a hundred percent of nothing. Then, when a claim pinches out, he sells it to some dumb greenhorn."

"If the claims are rich ones to start with, how come their owners are willing to sell?"

Conrad placed a finger on one nostril and winked at Morgan. "Now that's a real interesting question. I asked myself the same thing, and the answer that's being whispered about the flats is that Jamieson warns the claim owners that if they don't sell out to him they might be sorry. You heard about what happened to Slim Pickett, didn't you?"

"I did. He fell off a ledge and busted his leg."

"That's what folks say; some of them do, at any rate. There are others, though, who say Slim didn't fall. They say he was pushed."

"By Jamieson?" an incredulous Morgan asked.

"That matter's not entirely clear. There are those who say yes and there are those who say no. The ones who say no say Jamieson has somebody working for him. Somebody he pays to do his dirty work for him. Well, whichever way the land lies, Jamieson is sitting pretty. And I do mean sitting. He doesn't have to lift a finger to fatten his pockets. He sure must know some secret that nobody ever bothered to tell to men like you and me, Shad."

# SEVEN

The next morning as he was on his way to his claim, Morgan stopped short when he heard the sudden sound of loud shouting that was coming from a nearby ridge. He looked up, but at first he could see no one. A moment later, Jamieson came into view, starkly outlined against the blue morning sky that was made bright by the rising sun.

A moment after that, another figure came into view, and as Morgan watched, that man sprang at Jamieson, knocking him to the ground. Morgan sprinted up the slope to where the man who had downed Jamieson was now straddling him and savagely pummeling him with his fists. When he reached the spot where the attack was taking place, he pulled the man off Jamieson and shoved him aside.

"I must say I'm glad to see you, Shad!" Jamieson said in a shaky voice as he got to his feet. "That maniac was hell-bent on murdering me."

"Why?" Morgan asked as he stepped between Jamieson and the other man, who was preparing to lunge once again.

"That's why!" the man roared and pointed first to a sign that was lying on the ground and then to one that was nailed to a post that had been hammered into the ground.

CLAME NOTISE read the sign on the ground. BILL MACKLEY OF GRIZZLY FLATS TAKES THIS GROUND. JUMPERS WILL BE SHOT.

THIS CLAIM, DULY RECORDED, IS THE SOLE PROPERTY OF CASSIUS JAMIESON read the sign that was nailed to the upright post.

"He's a jumper!" the man who had answered Morgan's question yelled, pointing an indicting finger at Jamieson.

"You're Bill Mackley?" When the man nodded, Morgan asked, "You say this is your claim and that Jamieson here jumped it?"

"That's right, dammit. He's a slick son of a bitch, that Jamieson is. He plied me with the ardent until I didn't know which way the sun sailed across the sky. For five days, he kept me as drunk as a skunk back in town and then he comes out here—he's a jumper, Morgan. He's not a bit better than that thimblerigger you ran out of the flats not so long ago."

"Didn't I tell you, Shad?" Jamieson laughed. "You're a local hero. Everybody knows you."

"Is what Mackley says true, Cass? Did you get him drunk and then take over this claim of his?"

Jamieson gave a sorrowful sigh. "Philosophers throughout the ages have tried to pin down the nature of reality. Few, if any, have succeeded. I venture to state that no two men would interpret the same event in exactly the same way."

Morgan, growing impatient, snapped, "Answer my question, Cass."

Jamieson gave him an appraising glance. Then, sourly, "I'll answer it. No, I am not responsible for this man's drunkenness. Yes, I spent some time drinking with him in the tent I share with Maria. As you well know, Shad, when a man doesn't work his claim at least three days out of every seven, it becomes available to anyone who wants to take it over. When I saw that Mr. Mackley here was more interested in whiskey and a woman—I'm referring to Maria Almonte—I, after he had swilled himself into a stupor from which he didn't emerge for a stretch of six sodden days, laid claim to his piece of ground. I had it recorded in my name. It is mine now."

"You stole it from me!" Mackley exploded.

Morgan seized Mackley's shoulder to keep him from attacking Jamieson a second time.

"When I first met up with you, I made the mistake of telling you I'd struck paydirt," Mackley continued, his voice cracking. "That's when you started pouring the redeye down my throat."

Jamieson gave the sky a weary glance. "I offered to buy you a drink to celebrate your good fortune."

"You bought me a bottle!"

"I confess to what Mr. Mackley apparently considers to be a crime," Jamieson said piously. "I am guilty as charged of doing that very thing. However, Mackley, had I known you were embarking on a bender, I might have done differently. But as things have turned out, it does seem to me that buying you that bottle was a propitious move on my part."

Morgan wanted to look away from the self-satisfied smirk on Jamieson's face. Instead, he said, "Mackley, it appears to me that what's happened here is pretty much your own fault. When a man doesn't work his claim for three days or more at a time, it becomes fair game for any other prospector who takes a fancy to it. Those are the rules of the game as far as the Grizzly Flats diggings are concerned, and I reckon you know them. You ought to have gone a little easier on your tippling."

Mackley spluttered wordlessly for a moment and then, addressing Jamieson, "You, mister, better watch your step. I'll get even with you for what you've done to me. You just see if I don't."

"The street you're walking down has two sides," Jamieson warned in an ugly voice.

When Mackley, muttering angrily to himself, began to make his way down the slope, Morgan started to follow him.

"I suppose you think what I did was wrong," Jamieson called out to him.

Morgan halted, turned. "I'm not in a position to say, Cass. I wasn't there. I don't know exactly what happened between you and Mackley. But I'll tell you this. It has the stink of cheating about it."

"I broke no law," Jamieson glibly pointed out. "I had two witnesses testify to the fact that to all intents and purposes, Mackley had deserted his claim. I played fair by the Grizzly Flats's rules."

"Maybe you didn't break any law in doing what you did, but there's one rule—not one of Grizzly Flats'—that you broke. It's called the Golden Rule. What you did to Mackley I feel pretty darn sure you wouldn't've wanted him doing to you."

"You sound like a pulpit-pounding preacher,

Shad," Jamieson snarled. "That's a breed I have no use for."

Morgan, without another word, walked down the slope and continued on his way to his claim. By the time he was ready to quit that night, he had found several gold nuggets the size of peas in his sluice's thick sediment. Upon his return to Grizzly Flats, he exchanged the nuggets for forty-nine dollars at the assay office in the center of the shantytown and started wearily back to his tent.

After boiling himself some beans and beef and hungrily devouring them, he lit a lantern and proceeded to write a letter home.

> Dear Pa:
> With this letter I send you thirty dollars in bank notes. Yes, I have found some gold and hope to find some more real soon. When I do, I will send you some more money. I trust all is well with all of you as it is with
>
> > Your son,
> > Shadrach

He reread the letter, wrapped it around the thirty dollars in grimy bank notes, and placed it in an envelope, which he carefully addressed. After blowing out the lamp, he took the letter to the general store, where he bought stamps for it and was told by the owner of the establishment that the letter would not go out before Monday of the following week, which, the man said, was when the next mail delivery from San Francisco was due in Grizzly Flats.

He had no sooner stepped outside the general store when he saw the fiery forest of torches moving through the darkness toward the town. He was about to return to his tent when he heard the rumbling that came from the direction of the torches, a rumbling that grew louder and louder as the brightly blazing torches came closer to Grizzly Flats.

Men emerged from tents and shanties in response to the sounds that could now be identified as shouts as the torchbearers came closer. Faces bloomed in the light of the torches. Morgan recognized Conrad, who was leading the ominous group of obviously angry men. Marching in front of them was a slender young Mexican whose hands were bound behind his back. He walked stiffly, his head held high, his square jaw outthrust as if in a challenge, his black eyes ablaze with a blend of anger and alarm. His equally black hair kept falling down upon his forehead. He kept tossing it back as he marched on, appearing oddly proud although he was a prisoner. Blood slowly seeped from a gash on his left cheek and dripped down upon his elaborately brocaded jacket, which he wore above tight black trousers that were bound at his waist by a scarlet sash.

"What have you got there, boys?" one of the men standing near Morgan and squinting near-sightedly into the night called out.

"Ty Conrad's caught our gold thief," one of the men among the advancing crowd of torch-bearers responded gleefully. "We all helped Ty bring the bastard in when he sent word to us that he'd caught the varmint," the man added.

The crowd halted, forming a semicircle around the young Mexican.

"You can't trust greasers," a man on Morgan's left muttered to no one in particular. "Tricky devils, every last one of them."

"How'd you catch him, Ty?" Morgan inquired, his eyes on those of the Mexican, which, though fear-filled, never faltered.

"I heard somebody sneaking around the sluices," Conrad replied. "Figured at first it was just one of the boys working late. But I took me a look just to make sure. Well, sir, it turned out that it was this jasper who was sneaking here and sneaking there and taking any gold out of the boxes that he could get his dirty Mex paws on. So I collared him."

Someone in the crowd cheered. Someone else cursed Conrad's prisoner.

"He offered me five hundred dollars if I'd turn him loose," Conrad volunteered.

"No," said the Mexican in a steady voice, his black eyes still locked on Morgan's. "This, it is not true."

"Liar!" Conrad snarled and backhanded the young man, almost knocking him off his feet.

"Fandango," said the Mexican. "I come from fandango at Hernandez rancho. I do not steal gold."

"He ought to be hanged," declared a man in the crowd. "Now!"

"Let's do it!" somebody else cried eagerly. "Grab him, boys."

"Hold on!" Morgan shouted, stepping into the empty space between the torchbearers and the crowd that had gathered to greet them upon their arrival. "You men have got no right to hang this man."

"What the hell are you talking about, Morgan?" Conrad asked angrily. "No right to hang a gold thief? You're crazy if that's what you think."

"Get out of our way so we can get on with it," a torchbearer ordered, glowering at Morgan.

But Morgan stood his ground. "There's no proof that this man's a gold thief."

"You want proof, do you, Shad?" an irate Conrad roared. "Then search him."

Morgan approached the Mexican. He thrust his hands into the man's pockets, and when he withdrew them, there were several gold nuggets in them.

The men around him muttered under their breath, some of them pointing at the gold, others at the Mexican.

"There's your proof," a smug Conrad told Morgan.

The Mexican shook his head. "I never see that gold before," he protested. "I do not take it. Vicente Ramirez, he is no thief."

A man ran from the crowd into the general store, and when he emerged, he had a length of coiled rope in his hand. "All we need now is a tall tree to accommodate our Vicente Ramirez," he cried.

"Over there," someone said, and the crowd, like a river suddenly undammed, began to rush toward an aged walnut tree growing on the edge of the settlement.

Conrad, seizing Ramirez by the scruff of his neck, began to march him toward the tree.

"Stop!"

The men ignored Morgan's shouted command. It was not until he had fired a shot from his .31 over their heads that they obeyed his order and slowly, somewhat fearfully, turned to face him.

"Now then," Morgan said. "Are there any witnesses to what Ty says this Mexican did?"

The men looked at one another in astonishment.

"Witnesses?" Conrad bellowed in disbelief. "What's the matter with you, Shad? Have you taken leave of your senses? We don't need any witnesses when you yourself found the gold he stole stuffed into his pockets!"

"I know that. But still—"

"Still nothing!" hooted an irate prospector from the depths of the crowd. "Enough of this palavering. Hang him high!"

"No!" cried Ramirez. "I did not steal. *Por sangre mía,* I swear I did not!"

"*Cállate la boca!*" growled one of the men.

"What'd he say?" Morgan asked the man who had just spoken in Spanish.

"By my blood, I swear I did not," the man

replied. "You want to know what I said to him? I told him to shut up, that's what."

The Mexican suddenly tore himself free of Conrad's grip and made a run for it. Conrad went after him and soon caught him. He slammed a fisted hand down on Ramirez's skull and knocked the Mexican to the ground. Then, seizing him by the hair, he hauled Ramirez to his feet and gave him a shove that sent him careening into the grasping arms of the mob.

Conrad took the rope from the man who had gotten it from the general store and stalked over to the walnut tree. As he threw one end of the rope over a thick limb, Morgan cocked his Colt.

Conrad, hearing the metallic click, glanced over his shoulder. "You fixing to shoot me, Shad?"

"I don't want to. Neither do I want to see this man hang for something he claims he didn't do. What it all comes down to, Ty, is it's his word against yours."

Conrad made a guttural sound deep in his throat. "I don't believe what I'm hearing. Do you mean to stand there and tell me you'll take a greaser's word against mine?"

"I didn't say that, Ty. But what this whole thing boils down to, like I just said, is it's your word against his. Now that's a state of affairs that don't sit easy on my mind. I'm telling you, Ty—all of you—I can't see this thing through to the rope."

The crowd grumbled. Conrad swore. Morgan, his gun still in his hand, stood motionless. Ramirez struggled fruitlessly to free himself from the hands of the men who were holding him prisoner.

A tense minute passed.

"Maybe Morgan has a point," one of the men who had a torch in his hand then said to Conrad.

Conrad merely glared at him.

"I mean," the man continued hesitantly, "we've got no real proof—not any of the kind that would stand up in a court of law, we've not."

"There's no court of law here," Conrad snapped. "*We're* the law." He made a sweeping gesture. "All of us are. What we say goes."

The men muttered among themselves, and Morgan, seeing the doubt he had sowed among them sprouting, asked, "How many of you men are willing to have spilled blood on your hands tonight?" He waited, savoring the silence that followed as if it had been a victory, which it was not—not yet. "Blood," he added, solemnly, "that you might be able to wash off your hands but not out of your minds."

"It ain't right to let him go scot-free," someone whined.

Several of the men gave Morgan covert glances. He remained silent.

"He ought at least to be flogged," someone else suggested.

Conrad let go of the rope and muttered to himself in disgust.

"You got any objections to flogging him?" a man asked Morgan, and when Morgan said nothing, the man rallied the others around him, and within five minutes they had stripped Ramirez's shirt from his back, bound him to the walnut tree, and produced a black leather bullwhip, which they handed to a brawny man standing in their midst.

Morgan eased the hammer of his revolver back into place and then thrust the gun into his waistband. He winced as the whip rose and flew through the air. He stiffened as the leather landed on Ramirez's bare back with a wet-sounding *slattttt*. As the flogging continued, Ramirez, his upper teeth biting down hard on his lower lip, writhed and twisted in his futile efforts to escape the blows that struck him with steady and relentless regularity.

The sixth time the whip met Ramirez's flesh, his skin split and blood spurted. The tenth time the whip landed Ramirez screamed—a shrill, piercing sound. As the whip again and again found his flesh, he threw back his head and howled his agony to the unheeding sky and the thoughtless stars that filled it. He continued screaming as the somber men in the surrounding crowd began a solemn, scorekeeping chant.

"Fifteen, sixteen . . ."

"That, dammit, is enough!" an enraged Morgan yelled at the top of his voice. He bounded out of the crowd and ripped the whip from the hand of the man who had been flogging Ramirez. Shoving him aside and throwing the bloody whip into the underbrush, he quickly untied the slumping Ramirez's hands. He caught the moaning Ramirez as he started to fall and helped him sit on the ground.

"Go away," Ramirez managed to whisper between the painful moans that were escaping from between his lips. "Go away or I will kill you."

Morgan rose and stepped back.

Ramirez looked up at him, hate afire in his eyes. "I will kill you—all of you—for how you shame Vicente Ramirez this night."

Morgan reached out a hand to help him rise. Ramirez spit on it.

Holding to the walnut tree's trunk, Ramirez eased himself to a standing position. With his burning black eyes he impaled Morgan, Conrad, and all the other men watching him, one by one. "I come back. When I come, men will die." He turned and staggered, bleeding badly, into the night.

"There you go," said a man in the crowd as he handed some money to Conrad. "That's the thousand dollars I've been waiting to hand over to you if and when you ever caught up with our gold thief."

Conrad let loose a joyful whoop and, holding the money high in the air in one hand, proceeded to do an extemporaneous dance of delight. "Let's head for the saloon, gents, where the drinks will all be on me!"

As the crowd roared its approval of Conrad's invitation, Morgan turned away and started back to his tent. He stiffened a moment later when a heavy hand landed on his shoulder. Without thinking of what he was doing, his hand dropped to the butt of his gun.

"I'd be obliged to you if you'd help me celebrate my good luck, Shad."

Morgan turned to face Conrad. "I've not got

the stomach for celebrating at the moment, Ty. Not after that little show I just witnessed. Besides which, I'm in need of some sleep. Thanks anyway for the invite. Some other time, maybe, when I'm not feeling so squeamish."

They parted then, and Morgan continued on his way to his tent. He had almost reached it when he thought he heard someone moving stealthily behind him. He quickly turned but saw no one. He stood there listening, but he could hear nothing other than the sound of a fiddle's music drifting into the night from the saloon, which was followed by the desolate-sounding cry of a night bird. He was about to continue on his way when he heard a soft stirring. He squinted into the darkness that was partially dispelled in places by yellow lantern light filtering through the canvas walls of scattered tents.

He heard a sound he was sure had been a sob. Cautiously he turned and made his way in the direction from which the sound had come. Between two tents he found, lying crumpled on the ground, the source of the sound. He got down on one knee and put out a hand.

"Maria, it's me. Shad Morgan. You hurt?"

She shook his hand from her shoulder and buried her face in her hands.

"What's wrong, Maria?" This time he did not touch her. Crouching there beside her, he was reminded of all the animals he had seen in all the forests of his life, that had been run to ground by dogs or men and that, at last, could do no more than cringe in fear and whimper in despair.

"Go away."

Maria's words echoed in Morgan's mind, spoken by the remembered voice of a man this time —Vicente Ramirez. *Go away.* Ramirez, he remembered, had earlier told him the same thing.

"I want to help you if you'll let me, Maria." She shook her head and turned away from him.

Morgan reached out, and his hands gripped her shoulders. He felt her flinch but he held tightly to her and guided her slowly to her feet, although she resisted his efforts to help her. When they were both standing again, he took one hand and cupped her chin in it, raising her face to his. Moonlight fell full upon it, and Morgan, staring at the purple welt on her forehead and the bluish-black puffiness of her right eye, swore under his breath.

"What happened?" he asked as he released her. "Who did this to you?"

Someone coughed inside a nearby tent. The

sound caused Maria to start, her eyes darting wildly about as if in search of a pursuer.

"It's all right," Morgan assured her.

"I must go now."

"You're heading home?"

She shook her head.

"Then where are you going?"

She stood there indecisively, looking around, avoiding Morgan's eyes. Finally, "I do not know. But I must go."

"I'll see you home."

"No!"

"You don't want to go to your tent?"

"No."

"Why not?"

"I am afraid."

Understanding came to Morgan then. "You're afraid whoever hit you'll come looking for you."

Maria nodded.

He took her arm.

She tried to free herself from him. "Where are you taking me?"

"To my tent. You'll be safe there."

Holding Maria close to him, Morgan made his way through the night, passing a rowdy group of men who were passing a bottle from hand to hand, one of whom hailed him drunkenly. Once they were inside his tent, he lit his lantern and helped Maria lie down. He sat down beside her, and for a while, neither of them spoke.

But then Maria glanced shyly at him and whispered, "Cass."

"He was the one who hurt you?"

She nodded.

"Do you mind my asking why he did?"

Maria hesitated a moment and then, turning her face away from Morgan, she whispered, "He lives with me now. He takes much of the money I earn. He says I must do what he wants or he will hurt me. I fear him so I obey him. Tonight, in the saloon, there was a man named Rolf. I did not want to go with him because—the things he said—the things he wanted me to do—"

Morgan remained silent, his teeth grinding together, as the flame of the lantern flickered and made the tears that oozed from Maria's eyelids glisten.

After a moment, she continued, "Cass said I must—go with Rolf. When I would not, he hit me. Here"—she touched her forehead—"and here." She indicated her eye. "I ran from him."

"You could have come here—to me."

"I could not." Before Morgan could say anything more, Maria hastened to add, "When we and Cass were together—you remember?"

"I remember."

"I was ashamed about what happened. You saw how I went to him because of the money he offered me." Maria's voice dropped an octave. "You saw the kind of woman I am. I was ashamed."

"You can stay here with me," Morgan said. "Come morning, I'll go have a talk with Jamieson. Maybe I can straighten him out—if I don't kill him first."

Maria gripped Morgan's forearm. Almost violently, she shook her head. "You must not hurt him. It would only make things worse than they are now. There is an evil in Cass Jamieson. I see it sometimes—in the darkness in his eyes. He is a man with no heart. No soul. He lives only for gold—for money. He will do anything to get it. Use people. Hurt them. He is a man who can kill. I know it. Stay away from him."

Morgan said nothing, preferring to keep his own counsel. Silently he vowed that he would teach Jamieson a lesson, would pay him back for what he had done to Maria.

She sat up. Tentatively she reached out and gently touched Morgan's cheek. "I know I am ugly now—"

"You're not one bit ugly. Not to me you're not. You're a beautiful woman, Maria. You—"

Smiling, she placed a finger on his lips. *"Sshhh."* She reached for him, and in an instant, his arms were around her and he was crushing her to him, desire erupting within him like a volcano as the sweet scent of her filled his nostrils and his hunger for her inflamed his brain.

Morgan and Maria were just about to leave the tent early the following morning when its flap was thrown back and Jamieson appeared to stand, hands on hips, facing them.

"A man I know saw you two come here last night," he told them. "I've come to fetch her, Shad," he added, reaching for Maria.

"No," she cried, the word an anguished wail as she shrank from Jamieson's touch.

"She's not going with you," Morgan muttered, drawing his gun.

"Do you really intend to shoot me, Shad?"

"I ought to."

"I don't think you will, though. I don't think you have the nerve to do it."

The two men continued to face each other, neither of them moving, neither of them speaking. Finally Morgan set his gun aside.

"I see I was right," Jamieson gloated. "Underneath that rough exterior, Shad, you are apparently a man capable of some restraint. Killing me wouldn't solve anything. Maria wouldn't change. Perhaps she can't change. Perhaps it is something in her Mexican blood that makes her what and the way she is." Jamieson chuckled mirthlessly.

"Leave her be, Cass."

Jamieson ignored Morgan's order and, turning to Maria, reached into his pocket, withdrew his hand, and tossed something to her.

She looked raptly at the enormous gold nugget she had caught and then questioningly up at Jamieson.

"Rolf gave me that to give to you when I found you," Jamieson told her. "He said to tell you it's yours if you'll have him. And there is one more thing I must hasten to add. I will not deduct my usual commission for this particular transaction. In fact, my dear, I propose that we make a slight adjustment in our business arrangement. From now on, you may keep fifty percent of your earnings instead of the forty percent we originally agreed upon."

Maria's eyes widened and the beginnings of a smile lifted the corners of her lips. Then her face fell. Giving Morgan a sidelong glance, she held the nugget out to Jamieson. "I don't want it. Tell that to Mr. Rolf."

"My dear," Jamieson said wearily, "do let us settle this matter once and for all, shall we? Take Rolf's gold. Make the man—and me—happy."

"She wants no part of Rolf or you either," Morgan barked.

"Is that correct, Maria? Is what your would-be protector just said the sad truth?"

"Yes," Maria whispered.

"Speak up, my dear. I can hardly hear you. I must say you haven't responded with any great degree of conviction."

Maria opened her mouth to speak, but no words came.

"Shad, if you'll excuse us for a moment—I have something personal to say to Maria."

Morgan looked at Maria and then back at Jamieson. "I'll be right outside. Don't do anything you'll turn out to be sorry for, Cass."

Morgan, after leaving the tent, stood uneasily outside it for what seemed to him to be an eternity but what was in reality only a few minutes. When Jamieson and then Maria emerged from the tent, he studied her solemn face and wondered why she would not look at him. He glanced at Jamieson, who was once again smiling.

"Maria has something to tell you, Shad," Jamieson remarked, and when Maria remained silent, he prodded her with his elbow.

Still she said nothing.

"Maria?" Morgan prompted, feeling uneasy in the face of Jamieson's gloating smile and Maria's silence.

"Speak, girl!" Jamieson snarled, seizing Maria's arm and shaking her so violently that her teeth clattered.

"Damn you!" Morgan bellowed and lunged at Jamieson, who neatly sidestepped him as Maria cried, "Shad, don't!"

Her words halted him. Slowly he turned to face her.

"Don't," she repeated softly, her eyes downcast. Then, raising her head and glaring at him with a defiant look on her face, she said, "I go now with Cass. We have made—what is it called?"

"A business arrangement satisfactory to both parties," Jamieson replied.

"What does he mean, Maria?" Morgan asked levelly, sure that he didn't want to hear her answer.

"I must earn a living. Cass will help me do

that. He and I"—Maria took Jamieson's arm and fixed a defiant smile on her face—"we make one good business arrangement."

Under the onslaught of her words, Morgan found himself feeling as if he had just been stoned. "You don't have to go with him, Maria. You and me, we could—"

Maria's laughter—shrill, almost a shriek—pierced Morgan as she mocked him with it and with her contemptuous expression. "You have much money to give Maria?" she taunted him.

"You know I don't," he answered, keenly conscious of Jamieson's cold smile.

"Then what more is there to say?" Maria asked sorrowfully in a voice that made a mockery of that emotion. "Except," she added, "*adiós.*"

Morgan, as he watched her walk away with her arm in Jamieson's, cursed her, himself, Jamieson, and the world that in its sometimes savage turning, could tumble a man so quickly from heaven into hell.

# EIGHT

The next day, after giving the matter due and somewhat discouraged consideration, Morgan made up his mind. He sold his sluice to an eager trio of new arrivals in Grizzly Flats, abandoned his unproductive claim on the American River, and moved on in search of gold.

With a newly purchased sledge and pick over his shoulder and a supply of provisions in his carpetbag, he made his way east toward the Sierra Nevada range, with no particular destination in mind. He walked through dense forests into which the hot sun filtered faintly and made his cautious way into and out of serpentine canyons. Always his eyes roved over the regions through which he passed as he eagerly sought a glimpse of gold. By late morning, he was tired and still had found no place that looked promising to him. Sitting down to rest on a boulder, he dropped his tools and carpetbag and leaned back against the wall of rock rising behind him. Closing his eyes and letting his breath out with a soft sigh, he folded his arms across his chest and began to doze.

He was awakened some time later by the sound of laughter. As he sat up, blinking, he saw two men wearing sidearms rounding the bend in the distance and heading toward him. When they cheerfully hailed him, he returned their greeting.

"Have you perchance laid eyes on a man by the name of Emmett Howell?" asked one of the men.

"Not lately," Morgan answered. "But I know Emmett. You two're looking for him, are you?"

"We are." The man surveyed the area. "Old Emmett was in Grizzly Flats day before yesterday. At the assay office. He brought in over five hundred dollars' worth of gold. I was there and saw it with my own eyes. But Emmett's a sly one. He wouldn't tell me where he'd made his strike, though I tried my best to coax the information out of him. All he'd say was it was a rich one.

"Well, that was plain enough to see from what he'd brought in to be assayed. So when he left town, I followed him. I lost track of him about two miles south of here. But my friend and me, we're not giving up, are we, Billy?"

"We mean to find him," the man named

Billy said eagerly, rubbing his hands together. "And when we find him and where he hit it big, we plan on getting rich."

"Should you run into Emmett, mister," advised the other man, "you'd do well to stick to him like a lean tick to a fat hound and he'll lead you sooner or later to his strike."

When the men had gone, Morgan sat in the sun, thinking of Emmett Howell. So the old codger's gone and done it again, he thought with mild envy. Emmett's made himself another strike. He wondered if the profits from this one would go the same route as had the other money Emmett had made in the diggings. Lost at the gaming tables, according to the man's own admission.

His thoughts shifted to the two men searching for the gold prospector. Honey, he thought. That's what gold's like. It draws men like flies, me among them. He stretched and then got to his feet. Reaching down, he picked up his tools. As he did so, his sledge struck the boulder he had been sitting on and a jagged piece of stone fell to the ground.

"Lord a'mercy!" Morgan exclaimed out loud as he stood staring down at the yellow metal that his sledge had accidentally revealed. He dropped to his knees and clawed at the vein, scraping loose stone from its surface. The yellow vein continued.

Morgan rose, raised his sledge above his head, and brought it crashing down upon the boulder. The stone split, and Morgan cried out with delight as more and more veins were revealed. He kept hammering away with his sledge until the boulder had been reduced to a pile of rubble. Then he searched until he found a solid and reasonably flat stone, which he brought back to the site of his find, where he used his sledge to smash pieces of the rubble on the flat stone and then to pick out the gold thus freed and place it in his pocket.

He continued working, heedless of the passage of time and not even bothering to make a nooning. By midafternoon, he had two pockets full of flattened pieces of gold. Although the gold was malleable, the continual hammering began to take its toll on him. The muscles in his right arm ached, and the tips of his fingers, as he continued to separate by hand the gold from the stone that had imprisoned it, began to bleed.

As the sun began to drop toward the horizon, he looked up at the canyon wall against which he had been leaning earlier. But he could find no place from which the gold-yielding boulder might have fallen. He struck the rock wall several times with his sledge, but he found no veins of gold threaded through it. Maybe there was a stream here once, he speculated. A river, maybe. Water could have, given enough time, carried that boulder away from wherever it broke loose.

A thought occurred to him. Maybe Emmett Howell had found the original source of the boulder. Maybe that's how he hit paydirt, he thought.

"Hand it over, mister."

Morgan swiftly turned, his hand going for his gun. But his hand stopped in mid-air when he saw the revolver in the hand of the man named Billy, with whom he had spoken earlier in the day. His gaze shifted to the man's solemn companion, who said, "You heard Billy. Hand over that gold you've got in your pockets. But first give me that gun you're toting."

Reluctantly Morgan withdrew his .31 from his waistband and handed it to the man who had demanded it, the man who had been with the other one named Billy when they had earlier told him about Emmett Howell's lucky strike.

"We were watching you," the man continued. "From up yonder on that slope. We saw you find that gold."

Billy giggled. "Lem, he wanted to come down

here right away and run you off, but me, I told him, 'Let that fellow do the donkey work of getting the gold out of the rock and *then* we'll jump him.'"

The man named Lem tossed Morgan's revolver into some underbrush and then held out his hand.

Morgan reluctantly reached into his pocket, withdrew the gold it contained, and handed it to Lem. After stuffing it into his coat pocket, Lem again held out his hand, and Morgan again filled it with the remainder of the gold he had so laboriously extracted from the boulder.

"Turn around," Billy ordered him.

Morgan, anger flaring within him, stood his ground.

Billy fired a shot that bit into the dirt in front of Morgan's boots.

Morgan slowly turned around, and a moment after he had done so, he was brought to his knees by a vicious blow delivered from behind by Billy, whose gun barrel slammed into the back of his head, breaking the skin and sending sharp slivers of pain slicing through his skull.

The world grew dark, then bright with tiny lights of many colors that danced on the lids of his eyes, which pain had made him squeeze shut.

He tried to rise, but before he could do so, Billy gave him a second savage blow that sent him careening down into a black chasm that was empty of all light. The ugly sound of Billy giggling was the last thing he heard before unconsciousness claimed him.

He walked through a canyon, the walls of which towered above him and were made of pure gold. With a sharp point of a rock he had found, he carved his name in both walls: SHADRACH MORGAN.

He threw back his head and told the whole world, *"Mine!"*

From the rimrock high above him the faces of many men appeared. They shook their heads in denial of his announcement. They floated down to the canyon floor and began to fill the buckets they all had in their hands with gold they chipped from the canyon's yellow walls. Morgan tried to stop them. But he found that he could not move. He was, he discovered, rooted to the ground. He could only stand and helplessly watch as the gold he had found was swiftly stripped from the canyon walls, as his name disappeared from those same walls, as the men with the gold-filled buckets suddenly vanished like thin smoke in a strong wind.

"No!" he cried at the top of his voice, a futile protest. And *"No!"* again, a despairing cry that embodied his wrenching sense of loss and unfairness.

The sound of his own cries shocked him back into consciousness. He opened one eye. Then the other one. He was about to rise when it occurred to him that Billy and Lem might still be nearby ready to hurt or maybe even kill him. Warily he scanned the area as far as he could see. As warily, he shifted position so that he could see in the other direction. When he saw no sign of either man, he eased himself up into a sitting position.

His head hurt. He put one hand on it and felt the lump of hair that was mixed with dried blood. He winced and withdrew his hand. Then, picking up his hat, which had fallen to the ground when he was hit, he gingerly placed it on his head and got to his feet. He stood there unsteadily, swaying slightly, his vision alternately blurring, becoming clear, and then blurring again. He blinked several times and then steadied himself by placing one hand against the trunk of a tree. Gradually he became aware that the sun was below the horizon. Shadows lurked everywhere, imperceptibly lengthening and darkening. My gun, he thought. Got to get it.

He made his way toward the spot where Lem had tossed it, lurching along, his arms stretched out to help him maintain his balance. When he reached the spot, he got down on his knees and began to search through the underbrush, his hands doing most of the searching because his eyes were of little help in the deepening darkness.

It took him more than five minutes, but he finally found his Colt. He hefted it in his hand. He aimed it, cocked it, and imagined first Billy and then Lem in his sights.

In the morning, after a quick breakfast of boiled rice and baked potatoes, Morgan scouted the area until he found the tracks left by Billy and Lem. He proceeded to follow them, heading south.

He found the ashes of a dead fire where the two men had apparently made camp for the night. He hunkered down and put his hand on the ashes. Cold. He rose and continued his journey, his narrowed eyes scanning the ground in front and on both sides of him. He noted the broken branches on several trees, which indicated to him that the two men had plowed through a stand of thick timber instead of skirting it, which would have been easier but more time consuming. He noticed as he traveled on and came to a narrow stream the skeletons of several fish lying on the ground beside a pile of purplish droppings. Bear scat, he thought. A bear's been feeding on huckleberries awhile back and on fish just lately. He forded the stream and plowed through a dense tangle of huckleberry bushes that crowded down close to the stream. He made his way through them, eating berries that he picked along the way, and then halted as he realized that he had lost the trail he had been following.

He looked back over his shoulder. He spotted the place where Billy and Lem had emerged from the stream. He backtrailed through the bushes and saw what he had missed before—broken branches and crushed berries lying on the ground.

Those two, he thought, they sure got out of here in a hurry, looks like. They went running like the devil himself was after them. He soon found that they had veered sharply and headed back the way they had come. He followed the trail of broken branches and crushed berries back to the stream, which, he discovered, Billy and Lem had entered. But he could not, although he searched for more than half an hour up and down the stream, find the spot where they had come out of the water.

Angered by his failure to track down the men who had stolen his stake, he turned and walked south again, heading back to Grizzly Flats. He had not gone far when he came upon a pair of parallel ruts in the ground—a bear trail. He followed them, since they made a clear path through the trees and bushes, making the going a lot easier than it had been. He passed a red maple that had had its bark clawed up to a height of over six feet.

A few minutes later, when he caught the sickening scent of decaying flesh, he quickened his pace, his eyes alert as they hurriedly scanned the surrounding area. Grizzly, he thought. This here's his stomping ground, looks like. Maybe he's what sent Billy and Lem hightailing it out of the country. Back there he had his scratch tree, and somewhere nearby he's buried what's left of a kill he's made. A few minutes later, he came upon the partially devoured body of a young elk that was almost entirely covered with leaves and other forest litter. He held his breath until he was well past it because of the awful stench emanating from the rotting flesh.

As he came out into a clearing, he stopped in his tracks and stared at the startling scene before him. Prowling around a tall sycamore and snuffling loudly as it went was a full-grown grizzly, whose fur was a yellowish brown. The hump-shouldered beast occasionally stopped and looked up at Emmett Howell, who was perched on a limb of the tree above it.

Morgan's hand went to his gun but he did not draw it, since he was well out of range of the grizzly. His thoughts raced as he stood there trying to decide what he could do to help Emmett out of the predicament the old man was in.

The grizzly reared up on its hind legs, its huge front paws reaching in a clumsy, almost comical fashion for the man it had treed. Emmett got to his feet and reached for the next highest limb, but it was beyond his reach. He looked down at the grizzly, who chose that moment to let out a loud growl that echoed through the clearing and caused Emmett to try to shinny up the trunk of the tree toward the out-of-reach branch.

The grizzly's front paws and then its entire body slammed against the tree, shaking it. Morgan gasped as Emmett lost his grip on the tree's unsteady trunk and fell to the branch on which he had been standing. As his body struck it, it snapped and it and Emmett went crashing down to the ground.

Morgan sprang into action. He went racing toward the fallen Emmett, his gun drawn, his heart hammering hard against his ribs.

The grizzly, he noted as he ran, had dropped down on all fours again and did not seem to have understood what had happened. The animal was swinging its great head from side to side, its nose twitching, its small eyes blinking.

Emmett scrambled to his feet and made a dash for the tree, obviously intent on once again climbing up it to safety. But, before he reached it, the grizzly turned and lumbered to one side, placing himself directly between the tree and Emmett. Seeing its prey heading directly toward it, the bear grunted and then gave a series of harsh coughs.

Emmett screamed as it came lumbering toward him. He turned and ran in the opposite direction.

Morgan raised his revolver. Stretching out his arms and gripping the gun in both hands, he fired—and missed his target. The bear loped on after Emmett, its huge paws sending up showers of dirt and debris.

Morgan stiffened his outstretched arms to steady his aim. A moment before he fired a second time, the bear overtook Emmett. As Morgan's shot struck it in the right shoulder, the animal reared up on its hind legs and swung one heavy paw, which struck Emmett's chest and sent him sprawling on the ground.

Morgan, beginning to sweat, moved closer to the grizzly, unable to believe that the beast was still on its feet and marveling at the fact that the animal had shown not the slightest reaction to the bullet that had just slammed into it. He winced at the sound of Emmett's shrill scream and then swore out of a mixture of frustration and horror as the bear dropped down on all fours and began to maul Emmett, rolling the helpless man from side to side along the ground like some flesh-and-bone ball.

"Run, Emmett!" The words had burst unbidden from Morgan's lips, and even before he had finished uttering them, he knew that his command was one that the old man could not obey, because Emmett seemed to have lost consciousness. His body rolled first one way, then the other under the awful onslaught of the grizzly's sharply clawed paws. The old man's blood spattered his clothes, the animal's fur, and the ground.

Morgan stiffened and took an involuntary step backward as the grizzly suddenly raised its huge head and looked at him. His finger tightened on the trigger of his gun. The grizzly, as if sensing his intention to shoot it, abruptly abandoned Emmett and came shambling swiftly toward Morgan.

The sound of Morgan's shot split the air. As his round slammed into the grizzly's chest, the bear lurched to one side, shook its head as if to clear it, and then came relentlessly on. Alarmed, Morgan took another backward step—and fell over the exposed root of a cottonwood. His gun flew from his hand as he went down. He made a grab for it, but the grizzly moved between him and it. He quickly drew back and started to scramble to his feet. But before he could reach a standing position, the grizzly, growling deep in its throat, lunged snapping at him.

He managed to elude the animal's sharp white teeth but was again knocked to the ground when the bear rammed him. As its jaws opened wide and it raised one clawed paw, Morgan's hand plunged downward. When it came back up, it held the knife he had taken from his boot. Gripping its hilt firmly in his right hand, he lunged at the grizzly. His knife arced downward, and he felt it enter the animal's neck and then strike bone. He pulled it out and quickly brought it down again. The bear's snuffling stopped. One more blow and the beast dropped its head. Its tongue lolled out of its mouth. It shuddered and then collapsed on the ground in front of Morgan.

He got to his feet and stood over the dead animal, panting hard and sweating freely. He swallowed several times as he waited for his breathing to slow down and looked at Emmett lying so still in the distance. Then, rounding the dead body of the bear, he made his way to Emmett, fearing what he was about to confront, praying that the man was not dead.

Emmett was not dead, he found when he reached the old man. He hunkered down beside the prospector and spoke his name. His gorge rose as he turned Emmett over and saw the empty eye socket where the man's right eye had been. The face before him was awash with blood. The body was attired in tatters. Through rents in Emmett's clothes, he saw the clawed flesh that was red with blood. He saw the two exposed ribs, the almost completely severed left arm.

He fought the urge to vomit. "Emmett . . ."

The old man's left eye opened. "Morgan?"

"It's me, Emmett."

"I outfoxed the pair of them, Morgan. They

trailed me from town. They wanted—my gold. Didn't get it. Lady Luck was still on my side then."

Emmett sighed, and his eye slid shut as if he were too weary to keep it open any longer. "Lady Luck's a slut, Morgan. She ran out on me when I needed her most. She went over to the grizzly's side, damn her."

"She tripped him up, too, Emmett. He's dead."

"Dead," Emmett echoed. "Like I'll soon be."

Morgan wanted to contradict the words. Deny them. He knew he couldn't. Knew Emmett would know he was lying if he tried to do so. He said nothing.

"My pocket."

"What about your pocket, Emmett?"

"In it—my poke. Take it."

When Morgan remained motionless, Emmett opened his eye again and said sternly, *"Take it."*

Morgan reached into the man's pocket and removed a cloth sack that was tied with a piece of twine.

"She's with you now, Morgan, Lady Luck is," Emmett said with a sigh. "But watch out. She's a tricky bitch—not to be trusted."

"Emmett," Morgan said as the man's head

fell to one side. "Ah, Emmett, you poor son of a bitch," he said sorrowfully as he saw that the man was dead and that Emmett's still-open eye no longer saw the world that was alive with so many ways to trap and kill a man, grizzly bears being but one of them.

When Morgan returned the following night to Grizzly Flats, he headed directly for the saloon, which he found was full of patrons. He found himself a place at the bar and ordered whiskey. As soon as a bottle and glass had been set before him, he filled the glass and promptly emptied it. He refilled it and stood staring at the rough surface of the bar without seeing it, letting the whiskey burn its way down his gullet and into his gut, warming him as it went. He raised his glass again and emptied it.

Behind him a fight broke out between two men at the faro table and was promptly settled by the expeditious wielding of a wooden two-by-four in the hands of the faro dealer. Morgan paid no attention to the disturbance. Neither did he so much as turn his head when the sound of gunfire erupted behind him and then ended as suddenly as it had begun amid the wild laughter of a number of men.

He did start to turn around when he heard a

woman's laughter, thinking: Maria. But he stopped himself from doing so, telling himself that she was Cass Jamieson's woman, not his. No, he corrected himself. She's any man's woman. Whoever can pay her price can have her. Even old Emmett Howell could have her, he thought, were Emmett not lying in that shallow grave I dug and put him in before piling stones over it to keep the wolves from getting at the poor devil.

He poured himself another drink and was raising it to his lips when Cass Jamieson came to lean on the bar beside him. Jamieson watched him down the drink before remarking, "Where've you been, Shad? I haven't seen you in the last few days."

"Didn't know you were keeping track of me," Morgan muttered, feeling the fire the whiskey had kindled beginning to burn in his belly and spread its warmth throughout his body.

"I like to keep in touch with old friends. See what they're up to. How the world is treating them. How is it treating you, Shad?"

Morgan turned so that he was facing Jamieson. "How is the world treating me? Do you really want to know, Cass? Well, I'll tell you then. It's treating me fine. I've finally struck paydirt and struck it big, by God."

"Is that a fact?"

Pugnaciously, "You doubt my word?"

Jamieson shook his head. "Not for one minute would I doubt the word of a fine New England gentleman such as yourself, Shad. Where did this fortuitous event take place, may I ask?"

Morgan raised a hand and shook a taunting finger in Jamieson's face, clumsily knocking over his glass as he did so. "I am definitely not about to tell you—or anybody else either—that. That's my secret. I don't want jumpers all over my claim."

"I'm disappointed in you, Shad. I didn't think you considered me a man capable of jumping a good friend's claim."

"Good friend or bad foe, you'd do it, Cass, and not give the matter so much as a second thought in the doing of it. Just the same as you've been jumping claims all over the flats and getting hold of others one way or another without lifting so much as a finger to do an honest day's work of your own."

"You ought to go easy on the booze, Shad," Jamieson commented as he righted Morgan's overturned glass and refilled it with whiskey. "You look to me to be standing just this side of drunk." He handed Morgan the glass he had filled before continuing. "I don't jump claims. I buy men's claims, yes. I take over claims that have been abandoned—"

Morgan muttered an obscenity under his breath and drank from his glass.

"I've learned to pay no attention to a man when he's in his cups, as you apparently are, Shad. I think you're indulging in a bout of wishful and very fanciful thinking regarding this so-called strike of yours. Now why don't you tell old Cass the truth, which is that you'll be lucky if you have the cash to pay for the booze you've been downing so enthusiastically."

Morgan, as the finger of Jamieson wavered in front of his eyes, thrust a hand into his pocket and pulled out Emmett's poke, which he slapped down on the bar. "You want truth, do you? That there's the truth." Morgan belched. He emptied his glass. Pointing at the poke, he roared drunkenly, "Go ahead. Open it. Then tell me I'm being fanciful about striking it rich."

Jamieson hesitated a moment and then reached out and picked up the pouch. He opened it and peered at the gold it contained. Then, looking up at Morgan, "My congratulations, Shad."

A smug and intoxicated Morgan gave him a

lopsided grin as he took back the poke and pocketed it. "Told you I was rich," he mumbled.

"Cass!"

Jamieson turned and beckoned to Maria, who had just called his name. She came toward him through the crowd, a smile on her face, but when she saw Morgan, she halted, her smile dissolving.

"My dear," Jamieson said, "our friend Shad here has struck it rich in the diggings."

Maria met Morgan's gaze for only a moment before looking away from him.

"It's true," Jamieson insisted. "But our friend is being very secretive about the exact location of his strike. Well, who can blame him? The minute word gets out that a man has hit it big, prospectors come swarming like locusts from all over, and before you know it, the find pinches out. But, Shad, you forgot that once you file a claim, it becomes a matter of public record, so anyone who wants to can learn where you found your gold."

Morgan, his lower lip thrust out, shook his finger once again in Jamieson's face. "You're dead wrong about that, my friend. I don't intend to file a claim. My spot's one that's not likely to be stumbled on by anybody else. So there's no need to file a claim. If I did file on the land, like you said, half of hell's inhabitants would come swooping down on me once the whereabouts of my dig got to be public knowledge."

*Why am I lying like this?* The question ghosted through Morgan's mind, losing its way in the alcoholic haze into which he was slowly slipping. But the feeling that had accompanied it—half anger and half a profound despair—lingered to torment him. He sought in vain for an answer to his question. *Maybe I'm telling this farfetched tale to keep from admitting that I haven't had the least little bit of luck—lasting luck—where getting and keeping gold's concerned. Maybe it's that I'm starting to feel like a failure.* He turned his attention to Jamieson, who was saying something, his voice reaching Morgan from what seemed like a vast distance.

"—sure you didn't get it out of a sluice box or two?"

Morgan forced himself to concentrate on the words he had just heard in an attempt to decipher their meaning. Then, "Are you accusing me of stealing gold?" he snarled at Jamieson, his fingers tightening on the glass he held in his hand.

"Well, gold keeps disappearing from sluice boxes even though Ty Conrad supposedly caught the thief—that Mexican. Ramirez was his name, I believe. Now here you come with gold in hand and refuse to tell us where you found it. A coincidence, perhaps? Or something more sinister?"

Morgan seized a fistful of Jamieson's shirt and pulled the man close to him. "I'm not a thief. If you so much as hint that I might be one—" He pushed Jamieson away from him, releasing the man.

"Let's go, Cass," Maria pleaded.

Jamieson looked at her and then at Morgan. "Now that you're a rich man, Shad, perhaps you'll want to spend a small part of your newly found fortune on some pleasant entertainment. Maria's free at the moment, aren't you, my dear?"

"Cass, please—"

"For ten dollars, Shad," continued an undaunted Jamieson, "Maria would, I'm certain, dig deep down in her bag of tricks and come up with something really special that would be bound to please you. What do you say, Shad?"

"I say get out of here, both of you, and leave me be."

Maria gripped Jamieson's arm and led him away.

When they had left the saloon, Morgan

reached for the bottle on the bar in front of him. As his hand closed on it, an image of the badly mauled and battered Emmett sprang to bitter life in his mind's eye. He squeezed his eyes shut, trying to banish the horror. A moment later, he let go of the bottle and summoned the saloon keeper. After paying his bar bill with gold the saloon keeper weighed on a small brass scale, he headed for the door.

Before he reached it, Ty Conrad burst through it, his long blond hair flying, his brown eyes wild.

"They're coming!" he yelled. "Get your guns, men!"

The patrons in the saloon stared in surprise at him as Morgan asked, "Who's coming, Ty?"

"Greasers," was the shouted answer. "I was guarding the sluice boxes and I saw them. There were a whole bunch of them on horseback and they were having themselves a war council. I hid in the woods and listened in on what they were saying."

As Conrad paused to catch his breath, Morgan asked, "What were they saying?"

"They were planning on attacking us. They mean to burn Grizzly Flats to the ground."

"Why would any greasers want to do that?" a man at the faro table inquired skeptically.

"My guess is they're bent on getting even with us for what we did to one of their own," Conrad replied.

"You're talking about the whipping we gave that Ramirez fellow?" someone asked.

"I can't think of any other reason why greasers would want to raid us," Conrad declared.

"Was Vicente Ramirez riding with these fellows you ran into?" Morgan asked Conrad.

"I didn't see him. But that doesn't necessarily mean that he's not the brains behind the gang."

A loud shout racketed through the night outside the saloon. It was promptly followed by an even louder burst of gunfire.

"It's them!" cried a man who was standing in the doorway and peering out into the darkness. "It's the goddamn greasers and they're all toting torches!"

# NINE

Morgan, suddenly sobered by what was happening, ran for the door, followed by all the other men in the saloon. Outside, the crowd scattered, some to their tents for their weapons, other fleeing the area in fright.

Morgan and Conrad, their guns in their hands, took cover behind an adobe wall a prospector had built around his shanty to protect it from grizzlies. Both men began firing at the Mexicans who were riding through the settlement, lighted torches they were carrying held high above their heads. And then the torches, which sent seemingly animated shadows scurrying here and vanishing there, began to fly through the air. Canvas tents began to blaze. So did several wooden shanties. Gunfire erupted, coming from both the mounted Mexicans and the men who were struggling to defend themselves and Grizzly Flats.

Conrad suddenly sprang to his feet and ran toward a Mexican who was swinging a lariat as he chased a prospector through the melee.

When he came within range of the Mexican, he fired. His round struck the rider in the back, throwing him forward against the neck of his mount. The lariat fell from the man's hand. He leaned to the side, his left hand feebly trying to get a grip on his mount's mane. A moment later, having failed to do so, he slid from his saddle and hit the ground, where he lay motionless.

Morgan quickly reloaded his Colt and continued firing as flames rose around him, dimming the stars while simultaneously brightening the night sky.

Conrad returned and took up his former position. "Did you see that, Shad?" he crowed. "I dropped that bastard with my first shot."

Morgan rubbed his eyes which were beginning to water as a result of the thick black smoke that was swirling through the area. He coughed as he inadvertently inhaled some of it. Squinting into it, he was able to make out the figures of many running men. He found it hard to tell whether they were Mexicans or prospectors as the smoke shrouded them.

The firing continued. So did the shouting. Men cursed. They cheered when one of their targets went down. A horse raced riderless through the smoke and flames. As a bullet struck it, it reared, screamed, and then fell to the ground, where it lay with its legs twitching violently and its entire body convulsing before succumbing to the awful stillness of death.

"Ty, get as many men as you can round up," Morgan ordered.

"What—"

"Get them."

When Conrad had rounded up a half-dozen men, Morgan quickly outlined for them the plan he had formulated. "You four"—he designated the men he had chosen—"go down that way. You two, along with me and Conrad here," he told the remaining pair of men, "will head up that way."

"You think it'll work?" one of the men asked doubtfully.

"I'm hoping it will," Morgan replied. "The important thing is to give it a try. So let's move on out. I'll give a whistle. When I do, we'll all move. Don't try anything till you hear my whistle, else you'll be on your own and, I reckon, out of luck. It's going to take both bunches of us working together if this thing's to be made to work. Let's go!"

He was up and running and so were the other men, the two factions heading in opposite directions as they made their way through the ashe of tents and shanties, ducking bullets and veering out of the way of both mounted Mexicans and prospectors on foot.

A moment later, Morgan halted and held up a hand. Conrad and the other two men with him halted. Morgan put two fingers into his mouth and gave a shrill whistle. Then, beckoning to the other men, he headed back the way they had come. "Spread out!" he ordered, and the other men did so, forming a skirmish line. They began firing then, driving the Mexicans before them. When Morgan heard the steady firing directly ahead, he began to grin.

"It's working!" Conrad exulted.

They moved on, and Morgan's grin widened when he saw the Mexicans who had been fleeing from him and his three companions suddenly draw rein and circle their horses as the other four men beyond them attacked.

Then, as the firing from both flanks continued, the Mexicans slammed spurs into their horses' flanks and fled.

"Where are you going?" Conrad called out as Morgan sprinted away from him.

Morgan did not bother to answer the question as he continued his pursuit of an unhorsed Mexican he had spotted fleeing from the scene of the carnage. He leaped over the lifeless body of another Mexican and dodged between two wounded prospectors who were lying on the ground and uttering repeated appeals for help, their cries forming a pitiful counterpoint to the cheering that had just erupted behind Morgan.

He increased his pace and minutes later leapt upon the fleeing Mexican, bringing the man down to the ground. Both men rolled over several times, and then Morgan got to his feet. Keeping a tight grip on the shoulder of the man he had captured, he marched him back to where the prospectors were still cheering the victory they had just achieved.

He halted when he reached the smoking ruins of Grizzly Flats and cries of "Kill him!" and "Lynch the greaser!" erupted from many throats.

"There'll be no killing," he shouted, drowning out the voices of the vengeful. "I've got some questions to ask this fellow."

"What kind of questions?" someone wanted to know.

"Like who's behind the raid these Mexicans just made on us and why they did what they did."

One of the men in the crowd made a grab for the Mexican Morgan had caught. Letting go of his prisoner and swiftly stepping between the two men, Morgan gave the man, who clearly had mayhem on his mind, a shove that sent him staggering backward into the crowd.

A shot sounded.

Morgan spun around to see the Mexican he had caught clutch his gut and slowly bend over as if in a formal bow. He heard the groan that issued from between the man's lips, and he saw the blood seeping through the man's fingers. He watched helplessly as the Mexican sank to his knees and then pitched forward to fall facedown on the ground. He shifted his gaze to the smoking gun Conrad held in his right hand.

"I thought he was going for a gun, Shad," Conrad explained. "I thought he was going to shoot you."

"He had no gun on him," Morgan angrily pointed out.

"I can see that now," Conrad said sheepishly. "But before—I thought he had a gun. I was *sure* I saw one on him."

Morgan suppressed the urge to swear lustily. Fury and frustration warred within him, the second the sire of the first. He stared down at the dead Mexican, regretting the fact that he would not now be able to get from him the answers he had hoped to hear.

"I did it for you, Shad," Conrad said plaintively.

Morgan glanced at him, and as he did so, the fury subsided within him. "I'm obliged to you, Ty. I know you did what you did because you thought you were trying to save my life. It was a brave thing to do and I want you to know I really do appreciate it."

"Where are you going now?" Conrad asked as Morgan started to move away from him.

"After those raiders."

"I'll go with you."

"You'll not. Stay here and help the hurt. You and the other men had also best start trying to figure out what to do the next time those boys show up."

"You think they'll be back?"

"I'd bet my bottom dollar on it." Morgan went to where a riderless horse stood swinging its head from side to side in front of the saloon, which had escaped destruction. When he reached the animal, it shied. He spoke softly to it and then, after gently stroking its neck and nose, he swung into the saddle and moved the animal out.

He reloaded his revolver as he rode and then headed in the general direction he had seen most of the fleeing Mexicans take. He had been following the plain trail the men had left for little more than ten minutes when he came upon two men hanging from adjoining limbs of a sycamore tree. As he neared them, he recognized the moonlit faces of the two men who had robbed him—Lem and Billy. He rode up to them and, standing up in his stirrups, searched their pockets. He found them empty. The gold the pair had taken from him earlier was gone. Stolen, he was fairly sure, by whoever had hanged the men. And who had done that deed? He suspected that it had been the Mexicans who had just raided Grizzly Flats.

He rode on, a chill coursing through him, the vision of the two hanged men, both of them with their sightless eyes bulging, darkening his mind. Another vision replaced the first one: the Mexicans who had invaded Grizzly Flats, their faces orange and ugly in the light of the torches they carried. Dangerous men, he thought grimly. Men to be reckoned with.

He drew rein when he came to an expanse of rubble that stretched out as far as he could see ahead of him. No grass grew on the desolate ground. It lay barren in the moonlight, revealing no sign that any riders had passed over it. He realized he had lost the trail he had been following. He spent the rest of the night searching for the spot where the men he was following had emerged from the expanse of rubble-strewn ground. It was not until the sun was rising the next morning that he finally found what he had been looking for.

They rode west, he thought as he stared down at the hoofprints he had found in the soft ground. They used that rocky spot to change direction. They're trying to make it hard for anybody to trail them.

When he spotted a thin curl of smoke rising on the horizon just before noon, he drew rein, and after surveying the area, he rode on, angling to the left and heading for a stand of hemlocks he had spotted that was not far from the spot where the smoke was rising. Could be a cabin, he thought. Or a campfire. But it wasn't, he discovered when he was safely hidden in the hemlocks some time later.

He got out of the saddle, wrapped his reins around a tree trunk, and watched the Mexicans in the clearing beyond the trees as they made their nooning. Were they the same men who had raided Grizzly Flats? he asked himself and realized he wasn't sure. Several of the men looked familiar to him. Others did not. He counted the men. Then he counted the horses. There were nine men but only six horses.

One of me, he thought, and nine of them. Not such hot odds. He was considering his next move when he heard the sound of riders approaching the camp. Shifting his gaze, he spotted them moving in from the north. He stiffened as he recognized the man leading them— Vicente Ramirez.

He continued watching as Ramirez drew rein and the three men with him also halted. He heard the faint sound of voices as Ramirez spoke with the band of Mexicans. Their talk went on for a good ten minutes, and then the two groups parted, Ramirez and the men with him riding on.

They're in cahoots, he thought, Ramirez and those other Mexicans. I'd best be getting myself out of here before Ramirez comes back, he thought. He's got three men with him, so that him and his three plus those other nine—that would make for a total of thirteen, any one of which, I reckon, would as soon skin me alive as look at me. But he didn't move. He wanted what he had come for—information. He wanted to be sure of his ground before he made his move. He wanted to know for sure if the men he was watching were the ones who had raided Grizzly Flats, and if they were, why they had done so. Then, if it turned out these were the men—well, he thought, I sure can't take them all on. Not alone I can't. But if I can get my hands on one—just one—I could maybe find out what I need to know. Then I can head back to Grizzly Flats, gather me up some reinforcements, and make a move against them that's meant to get even with them for what they did to us.

His gaze shifted to where the Mexicans' horses stood quietly grazing, then back to the fire and the men around it. He waited. He was about ready to believe he would have to wait forever when one of the men left the others and made his way past the horses and into the trees no more than forty yards from where Morgan stood.

When the Mexican disappeared from sight, Morgan moved swiftly through the trees, making as little noise as possible, heading for the spot where the Mexican had entered the wood. His quarry was buttoning his fly when he reached him, and before he could make a move or utter a word, Morgan had come up on him from behind and wrapped one arm around the man's neck.

Holding the struggling man, who was desperately trying to free himself, Morgan muttered, "If you don't stand still I'll choke the life out of you, mister." The man went rigid. "Now you're going to tell me why you burned Grizzly Flats to the ground." Morgan still wasn't positive that the man he had captured and the men back at the camp were the ones who had raided the town, and he wondered if his prisoner would guess that he was bluffing.

"*Diós!*" the man managed to croak.

Morgan loosened his grip and repeated his question.

His prisoner remained silent.

Morgan bent down and pulled the knife from his boot. He placed its blade against the Mexican's throat. The man gasped and made a grab for it.

Morgan maintained his grip on it.

The blade, as a result of the Mexican's struggles, pierced the skin, letting blood flow down his neck.

"Keep it up and you'll kill yourself," Morgan warned him. "I won't have to do it."

"You will kill me?" the Mexican murmured, his hands dropping to hang stiffly at his sides.

"If you don't answer my questions . . ." Morgan let his words trail ominously away.

The Mexican began to talk. His words, a mixture of Spanish and English, flooded from his mouth in a torrent. Morgan, listening carefully

and occasionally asking a question, could not at
first believe what he was hearing—did not want
to believe it. Even when the Mexican had finally finished talking and had answered the last
question put to him, Morgan was still incredulous. And yet he was certain that the man he
had captured could not be lying, because he
knew too much. Names. And events that had
been taking place in Grizzly Flats.

Morgan returned his knife to his boot. He
drew his revolver and brought it crashing down
on the back of the man's skull. As the Mexican
crumpled unconscious to the ground, Morgan
loped through the trees, heading for the spot
where he had left his horse. When he reached
it, he freed the horse, swung into the saddle,
and went galloping back the way he had come.

He had been driving his horse hard for nearly
an hour when he spotted Vicente Ramirez and
his riders about a mile off to his left. He widened the distance between himself and them
before continuing on his way back to Grizzly
Flats.

When he reached the still-smoldering remains of the town, he went first to his tent in
search of Conrad but found it empty. He asked
a man nearby if he had seen Conrad. The man

shook his head and continued building himself a new shanty on the ashes of his old one.

Morgan headed for the saloon, which had not been destroyed in the raid although one of its canvas walls was badly burned. When he reached it, he tethered his horse to the hitchrail outside it and went inside, where he asked the man tending the bar if he had seen Conrad.

The man had not, nor had anyone else in the saloon. Morgan left and started back to his tent, but he halted when he heard his name called. He turned to find Conrad entering the devastated town from the north. When the two men met, Morgan asked, "Where've you been keeping yourself, Ty?"

"I was just out to where the boys are still placer mining. I negotiated myself a new deal with them. They've put up another thousand-dollar bounty, which'll end up in my pocket if I can once again catch Ramirez at his thieving."

"Then the thieving, it's still going on?"

"It is."

"You're convinced it was Ramirez, are you?"

"I am. Though I admit it might be somebody else. But after catching that crook once, well, I'm pretty well convinced that he's the culprit. And if it turns out I'm right—this time we'll hang him for sure.

"But never mind about him now. Tell me what's been happening with you, Shad? Did you catch up with those greasers you went out after?"

"As a matter of fact, I did."

"You did?" Conrad frowned. "You didn't do anything foolhardy, did you? I mean like taking them on all by yourself?"

"Nope. I didn't do that."

"Well, what did you do, then?"

"I cut a stray from their herd and asked him a few questions that were on my mind. He had quite a story to tell, as it turns out."

"What did he have to say?"

Morgan started to answer the question, but before he could actually do so, Conrad cursed and pointed. Morgan turned and saw Ramirez and the three men with him riding down a slope on the eastern edge of town as they headed for Grizzly Flats.

"Get your guns, men!" Conrad yelled at the top of his voice. "The bastards are back!"

"Hold it, Ty."

"We can talk later, Shad. After we've run that damned Ramirez gang off one more time."

Morgan, as Conrad went racing away from him, was forced to dive for cover behind a pile of wooden crates as the men of the town began firing at Ramirez and his riders and they immediately returned the fire, round for withering round.

He drew his .31 and surveyed the scene. Men were running everywhere. All of them, Mexicans and townsmen alike, were firing wildly. Morgan swore under his breath and then, peering through the thick dust that was being stirred up, found what he was looking for—Ramirez. He took a deep breath and then leapt to his feet. Leaving the safety of the crates, he dashed through the roiling crowd, dodging from a water trough to the charred door frame of a burned building and on to a tree growing at the edge of the town. His eyes never left Ramirez, who held a smoking gun in his right hand.

Morgan darted out from behind the tree and moved in Ramirez's direction. He lunged toward the Mexican's horse, reaching for its bridle with his free left hand. But Ramirez saw him coming and kicked out, his booted foot crashing into Morgan's chest and sending him flying backward, arms flailing, into the mob of men gathered behind him.

Morgan quickly regained his balance and turned to face the men behind him. "Take cover and hold your fire," he ordered them.

They stared at him incredulously. One of

them fired at one of Ramirez's men. As the man's bullet struck the Mexican in the right shoulder, Morgan swung his gun and knocked the revolver from the hand of the man who had just fired in defiance of his order.

The man cursed him and made an attempt to retrieve his gun. Morgan prevented him from doing so by kicking the weapon out of his way and then kicking the man in the shins when he persisted in his attempts to retrieve it.

"What the hell do you think you're doing?" roared a man Morgan recognized but whose name he didn't know.

"You'll get us all killed!" cried another man.

As if to prove the second man's point, a volley of Mexican rounds ripped over the heads of the men.

"Take cover!" Morgan yelled again and herded the men into relatively safe positions behind anything that would shelter them from the Mexicans' bullets. "Hold your fire!" he ordered them. "You don't and I'll turn on *you!*" he warned.

There was muttering among the men, and Morgan received a number of angry glances but he ignored both the words and the glances and went racing away into the whirling dust that was partially concealing other combatants, both townsmen and Mexicans.

He dodged a galloping horse, barely avoiding being bowled over and trampled to death by the animal. He ran between two townsmen, shoving both of them aside as he did so. This time, as he closed in on Ramirez, he quickly circled around behind the man. As Ramirez, unaware of Morgan's presence behind him, slammed heels to his horse and the animal darted forward, Morgan increased his speed, running as fast as he could. A moment later, he vaulted up onto the rump of Ramirez's horse, landing directly behind the cantle of Ramirez's saddle.

In one swift and fluid motion, he rammed the muzzle of his gun against the back of the Mexican's head. With his left hand, he reached around Ramirez and ripped the reins from the man's hand.

"Drop your gun!" he ordered as he drew rein and Ramirez's horse slowed. When the animal stopped, he dismounted, cocked his gun—and Ramirez dropped his revolver.

Morgan ordered him to dismount. Ramirez did, turning to face Morgan, his eyes glinting, his lips a grim line. Both men stood staring at one another for a tense moment as, behind them, an occasional stray shot sounded.

"Tell your men to pull back," Morgan ordered.

When Ramirez remained stiffly silent, Morgan slowly raised his gun until its muzzle was pointing directly at the Mexican's throat.

Ramirez shouted a curt order in Spanish. He followed it with a torrent of Spanish words. Although Morgan didn't understand a single word Ramirez had spoken, he did see and was gratified by the result of those words. The three Mexicans who had come to Grizzly Flats with Ramirez withdrew from the battleground.

Ramirez gave Morgan a haughty look. "You will kill me now? Me and my men?"

"I've not got killing on my mind, Ramirez."

"Ah, that is so? Then what, gringo, do you have on your mind?"

"March!" Morgan barked, and Ramirez marched. As the two men arrived at the center of the ruins that had once been a burgeoning town, Ramirez's men and a number of townsmen began to emerge from the places where they had taken cover. They moved slowly, warily. Their eyes shifted from Morgan to Ramirez and back again.

"You're the star attraction of this show," Morgan muttered to his prisoner, his gun muzzle still prodding the back of Ramirez's head.

"Let's hear it for Shad Morgan!" Conrad called out as he emerged from the saloon where he had evidently taken cover. "He's caught the ringleader of the raiders. Hip, hip—"

*"Hooray!"* chorused out of many townsmen's throats.

"Hip, hip—"

*"Hooray!"*

Before Conrad could lead a third cheer, Morgan held up his left hand for silence. "I got something to say to you boys."

"And we've got something to say to you," Conrad exclaimed happily. "You've earned yourself that thousand-dollar bounty, Shad, for putting a stick in that thieving greaser's spokes."

Morgan, ignoring Conrad's remark, thrust his gun into his waistband. "Ramirez, turn around." When Ramirez had done so and was facing the crowd of townsmen, Morgan continued. "This fellow's also got a word or two to say to you boys. He—"

Morgan, before he could finish what he had been about to say, was suddenly shoved to one side by Ramirez, who then tripped him so that he fell, hitting the ground hard. He went for his gun, but before he could draw it Ramirez bent and seized it. Morgan made a grab for Ramirez as the man straightened, and two shots sounded.

Pain raked Morgan's ribs on the right side of his body as a round ripped through his clothes and his flesh. He heard a woman scream, saw a man fall. Stunned by the impact of the bullet that had just grazed him, it was some seconds before he realized that it was Maria Almonte who screamed from where she stood on the edge of the crowd with Cass Jamieson beside her. Still more seconds passed before Morgan realized that the man he had seen fall was Ty Conrad.

He got to his feet, wincing with the pain the effort caused him, and stood there as one of the men in the crowd said in an awed tone, "He tried to kill you, Morgan. He had his gun aimed straight at your back. I saw it all just as plain. If it hadn't of been for that fast-as-a-cat Mex, you'd be a dead man right this very minute."

Morgan realized that the man who had just spoken meant that it had been Conrad who had just tried to kill him and not Ramirez, as he had at first thought.

"Why did he do that, Morgan?" the same man asked, looking thoroughly bewildered. "I thought you and Conrad were good friends."

"So did I," Morgan said softly. "So did I, friend." He turned to Ramirez, who handed him his gun. "I'm obliged to you, Vicente."

"I saw what he was about to do," Ramirez responded, pointing at Conrad. "I could not let him do it because of how you spoke on my behalf when most of these others"—Ramirez made a faintly contemptuous gesture that encompassed the crowd—"would have hanged me for something I did not do. I felt I must repay you for saving my life."

"And now that you've saved mine, Vicente, the slate's wiped clean." Morgan held out his hand, and Ramirez shook it. Then he turned and went to where Conrad lay. He got down on one knee beside the man. "Ty."

Conrad's eyes, which had been closed, opened. For a moment, he stared up at the setting sun, then at Morgan. "I had to try to stop you from playing out your hand, Shad."

"You almost did," Morgan said with no trace of bitterness in his tone. Then, after a moment, "You tried to kill me to keep me quiet, didn't you?"

Conrad nodded. "I figured you found out the truth. When you told me you talked to the greaser—" Conrad continued speaking for several minutes, and then his eyes suddenly widened as if he had seen either a striking or a startling sight.

Morgan watched them glaze as Death added Conrad to his many minions.

"I don't understand what the hell is going on around here," complained a man standing behind Morgan. "I wish to hell somebody would straighten me out."

"I'll be glad to," Morgan said, getting to his feet and turning to face the crowd.

# TEN

"First off," Morgan said, "I want to tell you fellows that you jumped the wrong men."

"Those greasers attacked us," argued one of the men in the crowd.

"These *men*," Morgan said with a strong emphasis on the second word, "did not come here to raid the town."

"They fired at us," someone pointed out in an angry voice.

"Who fired first?" Morgan inquired and was pleased to see the uncertainty evident on many of the men's faces. "I saw who fired the first shot," he continued. "It was him." He pointed to a man standing near the front of the crowd. "That's so, isn't it, mister?"

"Sure, I fired the first shot," the man Morgan had singled out replied. "I certainly wasn't going to wait around to get shot at before I set about protecting myself."

"Well, if these Mexes didn't come here to attack us, what for did they come?" another man wanted to know.

Morgan glanced at Ramirez. "I have a pretty good notion of what the answer to that question is, Vicente. But maybe you'd like to answer it for the gentleman."

Ramirez stepped up to stand beside Morgan. "We come here, my men and I, to tell you some truths, not to attack you."

"What truths?" Morgan prompted.

"That man"—Ramirez pointed to Conrad's corpse—"he is the one who was stealing gold from the sluice boxes."

Ramirez's statement was met by a babble of excited voices.

"It is true," Ramirez insisted. "I hear about the attack on this place. I hear it is made by Mexican men. I and my three friends go looking for these men. We find them. I say to them I am glad to hear that the gringos got what they deserve. Then they say with much pride that they are the ones who burned this town down. They tell me they are paid to do it by the man named Conrad, who—"

"I damn well don't believe a word of what he's saying!" shouted a man in the crowd.

"It's true what Vicente says," Morgan interjected. "I set out to trail the men who raided our town. When I caught up with them, I saw Vicente and his three men in their camp."

"He's in cahoots with them," someone yelled.

"That's what I thought at first," Morgan admitted. "But I wanted to make sure of the lay of the land so I caught me one of the Mexicans after Vicente and his boys had ridden out. I talked the man into telling me what exactly was going on around here.

"He told me that him and his boys had been hired to raid Grizzly Flats. He said they'd been hired by Conrad, who paid them in gold for their services. Gold he stole from your sluice boxes."

"Ramirez is the one who stole our gold."

Morgan shook his head. "Not so, my friend," he told the man who had just spoken. "After Conrad started stealing gold from the sluice boxes at night, he figured he needed a scapegoat to keep suspicion off himself. He ran into Vicente Ramirez one night—and there was his scapegoat."

Vicente took a step forward. "I make up my mind after you men have me whipped that I will learn the truth and when I do I will come here and throw it in your faces. Now I—and this man I am now pleased to call friend"—he indicated Morgan—"have done those things."

Morgan continued. "Conrad hired that bunch of Mexicans to raid the town because he

figured you boys would think Vicente was behind the matter because of the flogging he got,
and damned if you didn't. That raid would have
given Conrad the chance to stir you up all over
again and get you to go hunting Vicente—with
hanging on your mind.

"When he showed up here, you boys figured
he was about to cause trouble. Well, now you
know he wasn't. He came here, like he's told
you, to tell the truth about what's been going
on."

Jamieson spoke up. "What I don't understand, Shad, is why Conrad tried to shoot you in
the back."

Morgan looked down at Conrad's lifeless
body. He was silent for a moment before looking up at Jamieson and replying, "I caught a
Mexican during the raid. I was going to make
him tell me what was going on. But Conrad
shot him before I could question him. Conrad
claimed the Mexican was going for a gun, but
the man had no gun. At the time, I believed
Conrad had made an honest mistake—that he'd
tried to protect me.

"But before he died, he admitted to me that
he'd killed that Mexican so he wouldn't be able
to point out the part Conrad himself had played
in the raid. That's the same reason he tried to

kill me. Because I'd told him that I'd talked to the other Mexican—the one I'd caught at the raiders' camp—and he reckoned I'd found out the truth from him, which is exactly what I'd done. I was just about to tell Conrad that I knew he was the gold thief and the man behind the raid when Vicente and his men rode in and all hell broke loose, thanks to a few hot tempers and more than a few twitchy trigger fingers. Conrad also told me he planted the nuggets on Vicente—the ones I found in his pockets when Conrad brought him here the night you all flogged him."

An elderly man stepped out of the crowd. He hesitated a moment and then went up to Ramirez and shook his hand. "I'm sorry we misjudged you, son. I'm sorry, too, about what we did to you."

"We go now," Ramirez said to Morgan.

"Hold it, Vicente. One of your men got shot in the shoulder. He needs looking after."

"I will take care of him," Maria volunteered. Avoiding Morgan's eyes, she went to the wounded man and led him away.

Less than half an hour later, the man returned and he and the other Mexicans mounted their horses.

"We will find the men who burned your

town," Ramirez promised Morgan. "When we do, we will punish them."

Several men standing nearby volunteered to accompany Ramirez and his men in their hunt for the raiders, but Ramirez shook his head.

As he and his three friends were about to leave, Morgan said, "I saw two prospectors—two dead prospectors. I wonder, Vicente, if you might happen to know who hanged—"

"*Sí*, I know. It was the raiders Conrad hired. They told me they stole the gold those two men had and then they hanged them."

When Ramirez and his men had gone, Morgan helped to bury Conrad and then, as night settled upon the land, he returned to his tent, which he found still standing but burned in several places and badly scorched in others.

He lit a lantern and was taking off his shirt when Maria Almonte entered the tent flap and stood facing him. For a moment, neither of them said anything. Then Maria, in a soft voice, said, "I came looking for you."

"Does Cass know you came here?" Morgan asked, hating the harsh sound of his voice but unable to soften it.

"Yes," she replied with a note of defiance in her voice. "I told him I was coming here—that I wanted to find you."

"Why did you want to find me?"

Maria pointed to his wound. "I saw Conrad shoot you. I will come back with water, a bandage."

Then she was gone, and Morgan finished stripping off his shirt, wondering as he did so about the surprising ways of women. When Maria returned, she was carrying an earthen crock full of water and a folded length of clean white muslin. She told him to sit down. He did and then willingly submitted to her gentle ministrations, marveling at the sureness of her touch and at the fact that she had not and did not now shrink from the ugly sight of his torn and blood-encrusted flesh. She washed his wound, causing it to begin to bleed again.

"It is good that it bleeds," she told him. "The blood will clean it."

Minutes later, when the bleeding had stopped, she covered Morgan's wound with a white muslin bandage. He rose and reached for his shirt.

"You must go?"

Morgan hesitated.

"One cannot always live the life one wants to live," Maria whispered, her eyes searching Morgan's face.

"You sound like you're apologizing to me,

Maria. There's no need to. What you say's true enough, I reckon."

"It is for me," she said sorrowfully.

Morgan began to button his shirt.

"Have you found gold, Shad?"

"I've found some. Why?"

"Do not suspect me of thoughts I do not have. I ask only to know if you have made the dream that brought you here come true."

"My dream—it's not come true. Not the way I wanted it to. Oh, I found me some gold all right. Some of it was stolen from me. Some of it I spent keeping body and soul together. Some of it I wasted, like the night in the saloon when you saw me getting drunk."

"Dreams die, Shad. Has yours?"

"It's not dead, no." He managed a smile. "But it sure is pretty sick."

"You think of home—of going home? Many men who come here give up and go home. Will you do that?"

"Not yet." Morgan paused a moment and then, fiercely: "I can't go home, Maria. Not until I've struck it rich. I've got to make that damned dream of mine come true. I've got to find gold—and keep it. Not just for me. For the folks back home who are hoping that I'll make all their dreams come true along with one or two of my own."

Morgan was tucking his shirttail into his jeans when the tent flap was suddenly thrown aside and two men bounded into the tent. Before he could even turn to face them, one of them had seized him from behind and the other had torn his Colt from his waistband. Minutes later, his hands were bound in front of him by a length of rawhide, and a moment after that, both men were lifting him and carrying him from the tent. The last thing he saw before leaving it was Maria, who was standing and biting down hard on the knuckles of her right hand, which she had pressed against her teeth.

She set me up, he thought as he was borne outside, and he caught a brief glimpse of the sidearm worn by the man with the familiar moonlit face—Jamieson's. She led him and his partner, whoever that man might be, straight to me, he thought as he was thrown facedown over the withers of a saddled horse that Jamieson then boarded. Agony abruptly erupted within his wounded right side, which was now pressed tightly against Jamieson's saddle horn. Almost as agonizing were his thoughts of how Maria had betrayed him to Jamieson and whoever was working with Jamieson. But why, he wondered.

Why would she do such a thing? And why has Cass done me like he just had, he asked himself as Jamieson galloped away into the night, bearing his captive to an unknown destination, his partner riding silently at his side.

To Morgan it seemed as if hours had passed as the two men who had captured him rode on, but he knew that in reality probably no more than a half an hour had actually passed. He strained at the rawhide thong that bound his wrists as his arms hung down over the side of Jamieson's mount. It held. He twisted his wrists, first one way and then the other as he tried desperately to free himself so that he could reach up and seize his Colt, which was now in Jamieson's waistband, and use it to take control of the situation. But his efforts were unavailing.

He considered reaching up with both bound hands and trying to throttle Jamieson, but he abandoned the idea as unworkable. Jamieson just might shoot him before he could accomplish his purpose.

Jamieson's horse suddenly stumbled, and as Morgan was bounced against the animal's withers, he grabbed the saddle cinch and held tightly to it to keep from falling.

*Cinch,* he thought, the leather sleek and smooth in his hands. He eased himself forward slightly, moving cautiously, not wanting to attract Jamieson's attention at this point. He slowly stretched his arms until his fingers touched the cinch buckle. Straining hard, he managed to undo it.

Jamieson's saddle slid to one side and it and Jamieson hit the ground. Morgan fell on top of him as a result of his having deliberately slid off the horse. He turned Jamieson over as the stunned man fought hard to fend him off. He pulled his Colt from Jamieson's waistband and sprang to his feet. Holding the gun, he turned, searching for Jamieson's partner.

An instant before Morgan spotted him, the man fired the gun he had in his hand and Morgan's revolver was sent spinning out of his hands to land on the ground some distance away.

"Stand your ground!" barked the man who had just shot the gun out of Morgan's hand.

Morgan did as he was told, staring up in a mixture of shocked disbelief and bitter anger at the other horseman. "Jack Borden," he breathed, recognizing the crooked thimblerigger he had run out of Grizzly Flats some time ago and whom he had first encountered aboard the *Eagle* when the man was using the alias of Dr. White and bilking passengers of their money with promises of transportation across the isthmus to Panama City.

"My business partner," Jamieson announced as he got to his feet, dusted himself off, and retrieved Morgan's gun, which he returned to its place in his waistband.

"Birds of a feather," Morgan muttered. "How'd you two get hooked up together?"

"I had heard about Jack in reference to the thimblerigging game he was running," Jamieson replied. "The one you shut down—at least in Grizzly Flats. We happened to run into one another when I paid a visit to Rich Bar, where I had heard there had been a big strike. That was not long after I met you in the flats. Jack had relocated there, and he and I got to know each other and we subsequently formed a highly profitable business partnership."

Understanding came quickly to Morgan. "Ty Conrad once told me you were forcing men to sell their claims to you at a next-to-nothing price. Ty told me there were tales being bandied about that you let some fellows know whose claims you wanted to take over that if they didn't sell out to you they might get hurt. One was named"—Morgan ransacked his memory— "Slim Pickett. He was supposed to have fallen off a ledge, only Ty said there were some who claimed he was pushed. I take it Borden there was the man who did the pushing."

"I prefer to call what Jack did in that regrettable case persuading," Jamieson said.

"Birds of a feather," Morgan repeated angrily.

"Yes, I suppose you could say that about us," Jamieson agreed. "I suppose Jack and I are indeed birds of a feather who flock together. And you, Shad, are a bird we have brought here with us to pluck."

"What are you fixing to do to me?" Morgan asked.

Before Jamieson could answer him, Borden barked, "What the hell happened to you, Cass? One minute you were sitting pretty on that horse of yours and the next you were on the ground."

"This enterprising farm boy managed to unbuckle my cinch," Jamieson answered.

Borden gave a hearty laugh and then, suddenly sobering, said, "This is probably as good a place as any to conduct our business." He made a gesture that encompassed the tree-ringed and shadow-filled clearing in which he and the others were standing. "It's far enough from the flats so we're not likely to be interrupted."

"What are you fixing to do to me?" Morgan asked for a second time.

"This for starters," Jamieson answered and brought the barrel of Morgan's own gun down on Morgan's skull, sending him whirling out of the world and into one that contained nothing but darkness and pain.

Consciousness crept up on Morgan like a mountain lion stalking its prey—slowly but relentlessly. The darkness in which he drifted gradually lightened, and the silence that had surrounded him gradually gave way to faint sounds that grew louder as the light grew brighter.

He opened his eyes and caught a glimpse of the rising sun that was almost completely hidden behind the clearing's tall trees. I've been out for hours, he thought. How many hours? he wondered but didn't know the answer to his question.

He became aware of the fact that he was lying on the cold ground and realized that his hands, which formerly had been tied in front of him, were now tied behind his back. He sat up and saw Jamieson and Borden standing by a fire they had built. Their horses, he noted, were near the two men and they were neither hobbled nor picketed.

Jamieson held his hands out to the fire and then, rubbing them vigorously, turned around. "Our friend's awake, Jack," he said, and then both men strode over to where Morgan was getting unsteadily to his feet.

They stopped in front of Morgan and Jamieson said, "I had to put you out so I could tie your hands behind your back. If I hadn't you might have got the better of me."

"I may do that yet," Morgan muttered, eliciting a contemptuous grin from Jamieson, who remarked, "Not likely, Shad. There are two of us and all four of our hands are free."

"You try any smart moves, Morgan," Borden warned, "and you're dead."

"What's this all about, Cass?" Morgan asked. "Why did the pair of you tie me up and haul me out here?"

"I'd been intending to do that for some time now," Jamieson replied. "But you were off chasing Mexicans and so I couldn't make my move. But last night when Maria told me she was going to look for you and dress your wound for you if you'd let her, I figured then was as good a time as any. I quickly rounded up Jack, and when Maria came back for water and bandages and we knew she had located you, we simply followed her and she led us to your tent, where we probably would have found you on our own anyway."

"Then she wasn't in on this—whatever this is?" Morgan asked.

"No, she wasn't," Jamieson answered. "And as for your other question—we brought you out here to have a little talk with you. Specifically, to find out from you the location of your claim."

"My claim?" Morgan, puzzled, frowned. "What claim?"

Jamieson and Borden exchanged knowing glances, and then Borden said, "Cass told me you were spending money in the saloon last night like a drunken sailor and bragging that you'd struck paydirt. We made up our minds to take over your claim."

Morgan began to smile as he thought that the lies he had told about striking it rich while he was spending part of the poke Emmett Howell had given him following the attack of the grizzly had not only been believed by Jamieson but acted upon.

"After you tell us where it is," Borden continued, "we're taking over that claim of yours."

Morgan sighed. "We sure as hell have come a

long way from New York City, haven't we, Cass?"

Jamieson nodded. "A very long way, Shad, yes, we have."

"It's starting to look to me," Morgan said somewhat wistfully, "that I should have let you slide into the sea during that storm we ran into on board the *Eagle*. If I'd done that I wouldn't be in the fix I'm in right now."

Jamieson flinched as if Morgan had struck him. "I mean you no harm, Shad. Just tell us where you found color and we'll let you go."

"You sure have a funny way of paying back a friend who's done you favors, Cass," Morgan said. "I suppose you'll blame your pa for turning you sour?"

"Leave my father out of this!" Jamieson bellowed angrily. Then, in a lower voice, "What do you know about my father?"

"I know you think he doesn't—never did love you."

Jamieson blanched. "How did you find out—"

"When you were sick with the fever down in Panama City—you were out of your head for a spell. You said you were hell-bent on showing your pa that you were worth something. You were going to prove yourself worthwhile to him, you said, by getting rich. Well, what you're proving, Cass, it seems to me, is that you're nothing but a scavenger. You can't do for yourself—or you won't. You're content to feed on other men's kills."

"My father was a man who had a stone where his heart should have been," Jamieson snarled. "When I was growing up, he treated me like I was less than fully human. I learned to hate him. I made up my mind when I grew up that I'd show him. Somehow or other I'd show him. I made a vow to that effect."

"You picked the wrong man to use in your plan to try to make your pa love you a little," Morgan taunted. "I've got no claim."

"But you said—" Jamieson hesitated a moment and then, "I saw the gold you had in the saloon last night. *I saw it!*"

"Listen to me, Cass," Morgan said. "You too, Borden. There was a man I met name of Emmett Howell." Morgan proceeded to tell Jamieson and Borden about Emmett and about how he had come into possession of Emmett's poke.

"You're lying!" Jamieson snapped when he had finished speaking. "You're trying to throw us off the track."

"I'm not," Morgan said, shaking his head.

"What I told you just now, Cass, it's the gospel truth. I swear to you it is."

"I don't believe you," Jamieson snapped.

"Neither do I," Borden added.

"Well, the sad truth of the matter is that I lied to you in the saloon about striking paydirt, Cass," Morgan said.

"I think you're lying now," Jamieson countered.

"And we've got ways of making you see your way clear to telling us the truth," Borden added.

"Which is why we tied your hands behind your back, Shad, when you were unconscious," Jamieson said. "So you'd make an easy target."

Borden stepped forward as if on cue and threw a right cross, which struck Morgan in the gut. He followed it up with a left jab.

Morgan retreated as Borden's onslaught continued, unable to defend himself because of the fact that his hands were bound behind his back. He tried, not always successfully, to dodge Borden's blows or parry them by twisting and turning his body so that they landed harmlessly on his biceps or shoulders. But many of them could not be parried, and when one—a left cross—landed directly on his wounded right side, Morgan let out a sharp cry of pain.

"Enough!" Jamieson told Borden. "For

now," he added when Borden drew back from Morgan.

"Don't be a damned fool, Shad," Jamieson urged as Morgan bent over and gagged. "Tell us where you found the gold."

Morgan could barely hear Jamieson's words because of the way the blood was pounding in his temples and the pain was thrumming through his body. He could feel the blood soaking through the bandage Maria had applied to his wound and beginning to slide down his side, wetting his shirt as it went.

"We'll be generous with you, Shad," Jamieson went on, his voice a soft purr. "We'll cut you in for twenty percent of the gold we take out of your claim."

"To hell with that idea!" Borden protested. "He'll not get a dime. Besides we agreed—"

"Shut up, Jack!" Jamieson snapped.

Morgan straightened and stared hard at the two men facing him. "I think I can guess what you two agreed to. You agreed to kill me once I told you where my claim was. So I wouldn't be able to make any trouble for you two jumpers."

Jamieson began to smile. "So now you admit that there really is a claim—just as you originally stated to me last night in the saloon."

"That's not what I meant. What I meant was

that if there was a claim I'd be dead once you two had forced me to tell you where to find it."

Borden stepped forward. Morgan stepped backward. Borden quickened his pace, moving in on Morgan, who suddenly halted his retreat and, as Borden came closer to him with both bony fists raised, he kicked out at his tormentor, his boot catching Borden below the belt.

Borden screamed. Before he could recover from Morgan's blow, Morgan kicked out again. This time Morgan's boot landed on Borden's left shin. Borden screamed a second time and, with his hurt leg lifted, went hopping about on his other one.

"Stop it, Shad!"

Morgan turned to face Jamieson, whose unholstered gun was in his hand. "So you're fixing to stand up and be counted, are you, Cass? I wondered when you might get around to doing your own dirty work."

"Shad, you're making things unnecessarily hard on yourself. You're making this matter hard for me too. Now, Jack and I are reasonable men. We'll increase your cut to twenty-five percent. What do you say to that?"

"I say damn your eyes, both of you!" Morgan shot back. "You're going to have to kill me, Cass, because there is no claim and your bully

Borden there can keep on beating on me till I take my last breath but I can't tell you where to find a claim that doesn't exist."

Borden, whimpering, threw a right uppercut, snapping Morgan's head backward and causing his teeth to clack together.

Time, he thought, the word echoing in his mind. I need time. I have to stall these two or they'll kill me. Tell them I do have a claim. Tell them I'll take them to it. Tell them—

The series of savage body blows that Borden then delivered shattered Morgan's thoughts. He whirled one way, then the other, in an effort to escape the punishment that was turning most of his body into a terrible field where pains of various intensities did violent battle.

"You win!" he shouted a moment later, his head thrown back, the two words flung up at the sunny sky. "I've had enough." He dropped to his knees. He fell forward and lay facedown on an expanse of gravelly ground. Out of the corner of his right eye he watched Borden gaily clap Jamieson on the back and then both men happily shake hands as they celebrated their triumph.

He rolled over on his left side. He thrust his shoulders back as far as they would go. Then, straining as hard as he could, he pushed his arms downward until his wrists were level with his buttocks. Sweat beaded on his forehead and face. His muscles screamed silently as they protested the demands he was making on them. He concentrated on his goal to the exclusion of everything else. Above him the sky and the sun in it vanished. Around him the towering trees disappeared. The rocks beneath him vanished. *Do it,* he demanded of himself. *Now!*

He made one final full-bodied effort that involved, it seemed to him, almost every muscle, every sinew, every bone in his body. His hands slid over his buttocks, and he crooked his legs and swiftly slid them through the loop formed by his arms. Then he sprang to his feet, bent down, seized the first large rock that came to his hand, and threw it. It struck Borden on the forehead and toppled the man. He lunged at the startled Jamieson, seizing the man by the throat, rage alive within him as he attempted to throttle his former friend.

But Borden regained his feet, and with blood streaming from his forehead where Morgan's stone had struck him, he sprang upon Morgan, forcing him to release his hold on Jamieson's throat. Morgan slammed his right elbow into Borden's gut, which caused the man to gasp for air and release him. Then he went running toward the spot where his gun had fallen when Jack Borden had earlier shot it out of his hand. But halfway to it, he stumbled and fell.

From behind him, both Jamieson and Borden fired at him. Their bullets slammed into the gravelly ground that was deep in shadow, sending up small puffs of stone dust on either side of the prone Morgan, who leapt to his feet and ran on, following a zigzag course that he hoped would keep any bullets from finding a home in him. When he reached the spot where his gun lay, he bent, scooped it up, swung around, and fired a snapshot that nicked Borden's right forearm.

Got to do a lot better than that, he told himself as he swung his gun to the left and took aim at Jamieson, who was about to fire at him. "Drop it!" he yelled, but Jamieson, ignoring the command, pulled his trigger, and first flame and then smoke erupted from his gun muzzle.

Morgan dodged swiftly to one side and the round whined harmlessly past him. Both Jamieson's and Borden's guns were trained on him now, and he knew he could take one of them but he also knew that he would go down with that one. He shoved his Colt into his waistband and dashed toward the spot where the two horses were still grazing, apparently oblivious to the sound of the gunfire. He leapt aboard the first one he came to, and with his still-bound hands he clutched two fistfuls of the animal's mane. When he slammed his boot heels into the horse's ribs, it snorted and stampeded into the woods.

Behind him, he heard Jamieson's shouted obscenity and Borden's alarmed words: "We've got to get him, Cass, or he'll blow the whistle on us and we'll hang for sure!"

Morgan held tightly to the horse's mane as the animal tore through the woods, barely missing trees, leaping wildly over tangled undergrowth and tearing through thickets that stood in its path. Morgan ducked to avoid low-hanging tree branches, but he could not avoid the thorny branches of bushes that ripped his jeans and raked his boots.

He looked back over his shoulder. At first, he saw and heard nothing. But several minutes later, he heard the sound of another horse crashing through the underbrush behind him, followed by the snapping of a tree limb and a loud curse. Borden rode into sight aboard the other horse, his gun cocked and aimed at Morgan.

Morgan turned, and, steadying himself, drew his gun from his waistband and fired at his pursuer. He missed.

The sharp report of another shot, one that had been fired from in front of him, startled him. He saw Borden lurch in the saddle, obviously hit by the second shot. He turned and saw riders coming toward him across a meadow in the distance: Vicente Ramirez, with Maria Almonte riding behind the cantle of the man's saddle and clutching Ramirez's body as she held on to him to keep from falling off his galloping mount. On Ramirez's right rode his three men. On his left rode a man wearing a holstered sidearm whom Morgan recognized but whose name he could not at first recall. Then it came to him: Bill Mackley. Mackley was the man, he recalled, whom Jamieson had gotten drunk in order to take over Mackley's claim on the perfectly legal grounds that Mackley had not worked it for several successive days. When he looked back, he saw no sign of Borden.

"You are hurt?" Ramirez asked as he and the others rode up to Morgan and he studied the bruises on Morgan's face.

"Not too bad. But Cass Jamieson and Jack Borden have been giving me a hard time, as I guess you can see. How come you folks are here?"

"When I and my men returned to Grizzly

Flats after hanging the Mexicans who raided the town and murdered those two men—"

Morgan found himself marveling at how calmly—almost serenely—Ramirez spoke of hanging.

"—Maria told us you had been taken by Jamieson and a man she had never seen before. She showed us which way you went. We followed your trail." Ramirez drew a knife from his belt and severed the rope that bound Morgan's hands.

"And I came along for the ride," Mackley volunteered. "I happened to overhear Ramirez and his boys say they were riding out after Jamieson. I want him in the worst way for the sneaky way he stole my claim out from under me. He stole me blind and purely loved doing the deed. I've had me a strong hankering ever since then to get even with that no-good claim jumper, so I sure would appreciate it if you'd leave him to me."

Ramirez gave Morgan a questioning look.

"He's yours, Mackley," Morgan said and then forced himself not to ask the question that momentarily dominated his mind: *What are you fixing to do to Jamieson if and when you get him?*

"Now that the hounds are close to the hares,"

Ramirez said with a thin smile, "I think it is time for you, Maria, to wait here where you will be safe from harm. These hares it seems have sharp teeth."

"I want to go with you," Maria said firmly. "Like Mr. Mackley, I have a score to settle with Cass Jamieson. I hope he will let me settle it."

"I'll be happy to do that for you, Miss Almonte," the roughhewn Mackley said with surprising grace.

Morgan shook his head. "No, Maria. Vicente is right. Stay here. Wait for us to come back for you."

"But—"

"No," Morgan repeated and then helped Maria down from Ramirez's horse. Then, with a nod to the other men, he turned his horse and rode back the way he had come, the others flanking him.

"There," Vicente said only minutes later and pointed, drawing rein at the same time.

Morgan halted his horse and so did Ramirez's men. All five of them stared in silence at Borden, who was leaning weakly against his horse, his gun in his left hand and his wounded right arm dangling, while simultaneously trying to prevent Jamieson from boarding it.

"Dismount," Morgan said softly. "We'll

make less noise if we move in on them on foot. That way maybe we can take them by surprise and avoid any more bloodshed." He caught Mackley's eye, but the man gave not the slightest indication he had heard Morgan's words or, if he had heard them, that they had made any impression at all upon him.

"Spread out," Morgan whispered when they had all dismounted. Crouching, with his gun in his hand, he moved toward the two men. As he came closer to them, he could hear the hot words they were exchanging.

"You'll not leave me here, Cass," Borden was saying. "We'll ride out of here together or neither one of us will ride out at all. I'll see to that."

"You'll never make it," Jamieson argued. "You ride back here and what the hell's the first stupid thing you do? You fall off your horse, that's what!"

"I've lost a lot of blood. I'm dizzy."

"You're crazy if you think I'm going to nursemaid you. I'm getting out of here before Morgan gets back and starts blasting holes in both our hides."

Morgan moved still closer to the two armed men.

Jamieson shoved Borden to one side, and Borden almost went down. As Jamieson grabbed the horn of the saddle on the horse Borden had been riding, Borden kicked out at him. His boot landed on Jamieson's hip. Jamieson went staggering away from the horse. Borden, wasting no time, tried to climb into the saddle but couldn't because of his useless right arm. Jamieson went for him. Borden dodged out of the way and tried to deliver another kick but failed to do so when Jamieson suddenly and angrily reached out, seized Borden's booted foot, twisted it, and sent Borden crashing to the ground.

Morgan silently signaled to Mackley and Ramirez and his men. All six of them then moved quickly out of the woods, their guns drawn.

Jamieson, when he spotted them, froze, his hands still clutching Borden's boot. Then, as Borden broke free and scrambled crablike under his horse to take cover behind it, Jamieson fired. His round seared the air between Morgan and Ramirez.

"You do that again," Morgan snarled, "and I'll let light through you, Cass. That's a promise. One I'll keep. Drop your gun."

Jamieson hesitated, his eyes shifting back and forth among the six men facing him. Then, with a shrug and a joyless smile, he dropped his gun.

As he did so, Borden managed to climb clumsily aboard his horse from the right side. He fired the revolver he still had in his left hand, but his round plowed harmlessly into the gravelly ground some distance from where Morgan stood.

Borden's second round, a shot as awkwardly squeezed off as his first, also missed Morgan. It was followed by a scream.

Morgan spun around, and when he saw Maria stagger wounded out of the woods, he realized that Borden's second shot, which had been meant for him, had struck Maria instead. He turned back to face Borden and fired. Borden seemed to spring up from his saddle as Morgan's bullet entered his chest and stayed there. He let go of the reins and his hands flew up into the air. He crumpled and then fell from his horse, which trotted some distance away and then stopped, swinging its head around as if to see what had become of its rider.

Morgan couldn't help himself. He strode over to Borden, who was twitching on the ground. When Borden looked up at him, he put a bullet in Borden's brain that ended both the man's twitching and his life. Then he went to where Maria lay bleeding on the ground, a victim of Borden's awkward shot, which had been meant for Morgan but which had struck her as she suddenly appeared on the scene. He hunkered down beside her, put out a hand, and gently touched her face.

"You are angry with me, Shad? Because I did not stay back there where you left me? I was afraid for you and came to—to help if I could—" She coughed. Blood oozed from the corner of her mouth.

Morgan wanted to speak, couldn't. Could find not a single sensible word to fit the awful occasion.

"I died—"

Morgan wasn't sure he had heard Maria correctly.

"I died," she repeated, and added after a painful pause, "a long time ago. This it is not so bad. Only the good-bye I must say to you now—that is very bad. It is so hard to say it, Shad."

Morgan silently cursed the tears that were filling and stinging his eyes. "I wanted you, Maria," he said in a voice that broke. "I didn't want you to go back to Cass."

Her hand rose and came to rest on Morgan's cheek. "I had to."

"I don't understand."

"You remember when Cass asked to speak to me alone that morning in the tent, and you went outside so he could do so?" When Morgan nodded, Maria continued. "He told me he would hurt you, maybe kill you, if I did not come back to him. I did not want anything bad to happen to you. So I went with him."

"I didn't know," Morgan said, his voice cracking.

"He promised me he would not hurt you as long as I stayed with him—and did what he told me to do. But when he and the other man with him took you away—" Maria's eyes squeezed shut and then opened again. She shuddered. "I knew he had broken his word to me. I knew I had to do something to try to help you. Then Vicente Ramirez came to town and I—I told him—"

"Try to take it easy, Maria," Morgan whispered.

Maria's hand fell away from Morgan's face. "Tell me a lie, Shad," she breathed, the words coming huskily from between her lips. "Tell me you loved me."

Morgan swallowed once, twice. Then, "I loved—love you, Maria," he said and knew it was no lie.

As life left Maria, Jamieson made his move. He quickly retrieved the gun he had earlier been forced to drop, and clutching it in both hands and cursing Morgan at the top of his voice . . .

Mackley shot him between the eyes before he could fire.

Jamieson staggered back a few steps. His fingers splayed out and the gun fell from his hands. He went down to lie motionless on the hard gravelly ground.

Morgan was about to turn away from him when the sun topped the trees and he saw the glow of yellow metal embedded in the bullet-nicked gravel on both sides of Jamieson's corpse that had earlier been hidden by the shadows shed by the trees.

He got down on one knee. He put out a hand. He picked up a handful of gravel—and the gold it contained. He looked up at Ramirez.

Ramirez smiled down at him. "You have found much gold, Morgan. See there where bullets have revealed it to you like a marvelous secret the ground could no longer keep."

Morgan looked down and then began to claw almost frantically at the ground. He uncovered more gold, a thick vein of it lying less than five inches below the surface. He pulled his knife from his boot and began to gouge the ground with it. The deeper he dug the more gold he discovered. He sprang to his feet and was about to give a triumphant cry when his eyes happened to fall on Jamieson's corpse. His gaze shifted to Borden's lifeless body and then to Maria's.

Ramirez came up to him and put a comforting hand on his shoulder. "Gold," he said softly, "it is like a path with many turnings. Some men, they lose their way as they follow it. Others—men like you—do not. It is very sad what gold can do to some men." Ramirez indicated Jamieson's and Borden's bodies. "Or to some women." He glanced at Maria, lying lifeless in the sun that would never again warm her.

Morgan turned away.

"It is not gold that does the bad things," Ramirez pointed out to him. "It is people who do the bad things. Like those two who did evil to get gold." Again he indicated Jamieson and Borden.

"Maria was tricked by gold," Morgan said softly. "She saw it as the only way to the good life, and what it got her in the end was death."

"It is—how do you say—ironic?" Ramirez smiled. "Those two bad men bring you here, and here, when they are gone, you find gold."

"I mean to share it with you and your men, Vicente," Morgan said. "And with you too," he told Mackley, who was standing nearby.

They all shook their heads. Ramirez said, "You were here first. It is your strike."

"And make no mistake about it, we're no claim jumpers," Mackley added with a grin.

Morgan turned around and looked down at the treasure he had found at his feet, and this time he could not help himself. He gave a loud shout of pure joy and then another even louder one.